THE VENDETTI
Queen

CAPO DEI CAPI RUTHLESS
MATTEO VENDETTI

INTERNATIONAL BESTSELLING AUTHOR
SAPPHIRE KNIGHT

The Vendetti Queen

www.authorsapphireknight.com

THE VENDETTI Queen

CAPO DEI CAPI RUTHLESS
MATTEO VENDETTI

INTERNATIONAL BESTSELLING AUTHOR

SAPPHIRE KNIGHT

.

The Vendetti Queen

Copyright © 2019 by Sapphire Knight

Cover Design by CT Cover Creations

Editing by Brandi Salazar

Format by

WARNING

This novel includes graphic language and adult situations. It may be offensive to some readers and includes situations that may be hotspots for certain individuals. This book is intended for ages 17 and older due to some steamy spots. **This work is fictional.** The story is meant to entertain the reader and may not always be completely accurate. Any reproduction of these works without Author Sapphire Knight's written consent is pirating and will be punished to the fullest extent of the law.

This book is fiction.

The guys are over the top Alphas.

My men and women are nuts.

This is not real.

Don't steal my shit.

Read for enjoyment.

This is not your momma's cookbook.

Easily offended people should not read this.

Don't be a dick.

Acknowledgements

My husband - I love you more than words can express. Thank you for the support you've shown me. Some days you drive me crazy, other days I just want to kiss your face off. Who knew this would turn out to be our life, but in this journey, I wouldn't want to spend it with anyone else. Thanks for falling for my brand of crazy. I love you, I'm thankful for you, I can't say it enough.

My boys - You are my whole world. I love you both. This never changes, and you better not be reading these books until you're thirty and tell yourself your momma did not write them! I can never express how grateful I am for your support. You are quick to tell me that my career makes you proud, that I make you proud. As far as mom wins go; that one takes the cake. I love you with every beat of my heart and I will forever.

My Beta Babes - This wouldn't be possible without you. I can't express my gratitude enough for each of you. Thank you so much!

Editor Brandi Salazar – Your hard work makes mine stand out, and I'm so grateful! Thank you for pouring tons of hours into my passion and being so wonderful to me. Thank you for your friendship and support.

Cover Designer Clarise Tan– I cannot thank you enough for the wonderful work you've done for me. Your support truly means so much. I can't wait to see our future projects, you always blow me away. You are a creative genius!

Photographer and Cover Model Gigi Hoggard - Thank you so much for the support you've been kind enough to show me in our book community. Your talent is beyond amazing and I look forward to our future projects. You've made the entire process quick and easy. Thank you for your friendship and for sharing your amazing ability to adapt to what I needed. I adore you and am over the moon with you being The Queen.

Formatting – Thank you so much for making my books always look professional and beautiful. I truly appreciate it and the kindness you've shown me. I know I can depend on you even in short notice and it's so refreshing. You are always quick and efficient, thank you!!!

My good friends Hilary Storm and Victoria Ashley - Thank you for being supportive and always giving it to me straight. My life is better with you two in it! #Crew

My Blogger Friends –YOU ARE AMAZING! I LOVE YOU! No really, I do!!! You take a new chance on me with each book and in return share my passion with the world. You never truly get enough credit, and I'm forever grateful!

My Readers – I love you. You make my life possible, thank you. I can't wait to meet many of you this year and in the future!

Also By Sapphire:

Oath Keepers MC Series
Secrets
Exposed
Relinquish
Forsaken Control
Friction
Princess
Sweet Surrender – free short story
Love and Obey – free short story
Daydream
Baby
Chevelle
Cherry

Russkaya Mafiya Series
Secrets
Corrupted
Corrupted Counterparts – free short story
Unwanted Sacrifices
Undercover Intentions

Dirty Down South Series
1st Time Love
3 Times the Heat

Complete Standalones
Gangster
Unexpected Forfeit
The Main Event – free short story
Oath Keepers MC Collection
Russian Roulette

Tease – Short Story Collection
Oath Keepers MC Hybrid Collection

Capo Dei Capi Vendetti
The Vendetti Empire - part 1
The Vendetti Queen - part 2

Dedicated to:

The readers who skipped the warning.
You rebel.
Now, let's hope you don't shit your pants because of it.

Common terms:

Capo dei Capi – Boss of bosses
Polizia – Police
Mia - My
Familia – Family
Bella – Beautiful
Moglie – Wife
Fidanzata – Fiancé
Fiore – Flower
Violetta – Violet
Grazie – Thanks
Si- Yes

Vendetti Familia Structure

Romano and Liliana Vendetti – Parents

Matteo 'Ruthless' Vendetti (33) – 1st and Capo dei capi, head of the familia

Violet Vendetti (19) – Wife to Matteo and the Vendetti Queen

Salvatore Vendetti (30) – 2nd

Valentino Vendetti (27) – 3rd

Dante Vendetti (24) – 4th

Luciano Vendetti (21) – 5th

Santino Vendetti (18) – 6th

Cristiano Vendetti (17) – 7th

From Part 1

I love the smell of don't fuck with me in the morning.

- theclassypeople

Violet

My thighs clench wantonly at Cristiano's confession and the delicious burn I'm met with reminds me of Santino's thickness being there earlier. My core's still recovering from our time together in the coat closet. I'll never be able to return there without remembering of how his length filled me and how Matteo's penetrating gaze bore into mine as I gave into the ecstasy. Now it's Cristiano's turn and I can't help but wonder if his size is anything close to Santino or Matteo or even Dante. I don't know if I'll make it through tonight if that's the case, no matter how turned on I am or want to please Matteo by doing this for him and his family.

Matteo's here watching me and I'm going to disappoint him, if that's the case. Will he punish me in his office if I speak up against being fucked again? I'd never have imagined I'd have such a powerful man like my husband Matteo or that I'd be intimate with all of the Vendetti's in line to fill the shoes of Capo.

I've never been one not to speak up, the consequences be damned. To think, in the beginning all I wanted was a man to know how to touch me, to make me feel. I've gotten my wish, plus bitten off way more than I can possibly chew.

Cristiano pauses in his perusal and a throat clears. The sound comes from none other than my husband. "Mia fiore, what is it? You're stiff as a board. You need to relax."

His rasp does funny things to my stomach, the flip flop telling me that I want him above any others. I've never felt so out of control; utterly owned and inexperienced as to when it comes to being next to that man. The things he does to me...

Drawing in a breath, I confess, "I'm a bit sore." It takes all of my courage to admit it to him and in front of his younger brother as witness. He told me he'd bend me to his will and that I'll obey, but I won't lie to him about any of it or how I feel.

A finger presses against my clit through my satin panties and his voice deepens if that's even possible. "Your pussy hurts? It was fucked too hard?"

Jerking my head, I silently nod even though his finger feels amazing touching me.

I can't see him, but a low groan sounds in his throat telling me he definitely saw me. The rooms so quiet I can hear myself breathing. A few beats pass with me shifting to press my legs together again as his finger circles my clit. I may be sore, but I still want to please him.

He curses, finally muttering for me to turn on my side. I do as he says, moving the scrap of panties off before getting comfy, so he knows I want to continue to be touched. One hand slides under the pillow, the other laying on my hip, I wait.

The bed dips behind me as Cristiano slides back to the same spot that he'd woken me up in. His hand glides over the round globe of my butt, the palm size seemingly much bigger than I'd imagined. Matteo has large, capable hands; Cristiano must mimic him in that as well. His finger stops at the bottom, tracing the area where the crease meets the back of my thigh. His breaths increase, the warmth fluttering against my neck as he caresses the line again and my body squirms in anticipation.

His lips meet my neck, beginning the exploration anew as the tips of two fingers sneak between the juncture of my thighs. They carefully brush my sex, applying enough pressure to feel the moisture pooling. Cristiano's careful not to rub too roughly, my flesh swelling and opening for him. My body wants the pleasure, and as the tips penetrate me a few inches my core clenches, attempting to draw him in.

He's so quiet, unlike his brothers; he gives nothing away at how he's feeling. The silence has me off balance, if it weren't for his eager touch and his warm kisses, I'd wonder if I was dreaming this entire night. His muscular thigh moves mine upwards, pinning me down as he sees fit. Cristiano guides himself to my core, the rounded head meeting my opening. He moves his cock gently brushing me as he'd done moments prior with his fingers. My breasts heave as I get more and more turned on for him, knowing Matteo is right here with us as well.

Another caress from the silken tip and an impatient cry breaks free. My pussy clenches so tightly, as if it will grip his cock and pull it inside. I thought I was too sore, but I want him in me far more than him to stop.

"You ready for me?" He murmurs, his voice sounding as if it's in front of me rather than behind but I know that can't be the case.

I'm too focused on my need to care about the details and confess, "Yes, I want it."

"What do you want, beautiful?" Cristiano murmurs and I groan with frustration.

"Your cock, if you're going to keep teasing me, let Matteo just fuck me already."

A growl sounds from behind, teeth sinking into the back of my neck as his cock thrusts deep.

"Oh!" I call in surprise.

A hand finds my hair, gripping the locks, he yanks my head back to bite my neck harder and thrusts in again, both hitting me at the same time.

"Fuck me!" I can't help but yell loudly. Cristiano may end up being the best out of all at this point. The pain holding me back from minutes before has escaped my body completely, as all I can think of is having him deeper in me.

His other hand grabs my thigh, the thickness a natural grip for his powerful drive. The hold is firmer than I'd expect, he keeps me off kilter as to what he'll do. So much for soft and sweet, the man is going to ride me until I break from too many orgasms. A growl into my neck has chills flaring over my body, the heat spreading like wild fire, "Oh, I'll fuck you alright." The raspy reply sounds more like an angry promise from Matteo, rather than his brother Cristiano, further confusing my mind and body.

The moans leave me in screams ridiculously loud. I wouldn't be too stunned if his brothers burst in here. The insane sensations of his cock plunging into my core, pounding me into oblivion have me seeing stars. I can barely catch my breath as once he begins, he's like a machine, taking over and possessing me with his movements. Each drive has his length pressing exactly where I need him to. His hips thrust his dick in and out, again and again; the pressure repeatedly hitting my g-spot has me begging for the release.

"Oh, shit! Please Crisitano!"

His answering groan and throbbing cock have me matching him pulse for pulse. I want to turn over, hold him down and ride him into unconsciousness. I don't know if these Vendetti's could handle the lack of control though, especially my husband.

"So perfect," the man behind me whispers. His firm chest brushes my back as his breathing slows to eager, pleased pants. Feeling his excitement surround me, only feeds into my own and my body erupts. I'm lost, tumbling down a deep bottomless hole as ecstasy grips me, turning me inside out. One demanding yank on my hair has me letting go entirely, screaming my release.

The orgasm washes over me, exhausting what diminutive amount of energy I'd recovered from my brief nap. As he moans through his own pleasure, my body relinquishes into a pile of overused, worn out muscles. The eventful evening along with the attention and utopia offered mixed with too much champagne has me knocked on my ass. It's as if I've just run a marathon and could slumber for a week... yet, this is my life now.

Being a Bottaro was not boring, but it definitely wasn't like this.

Matteo

1 week later...

I'm done sharing her.

The tradition required for me to give her to my brothers and for us to attempt to impregnate her immediately. We each did our part and now she can finally become mine. Thank fuck, as much as I love my brothers, I don't enjoy sharing mia Violetta, my perfect little flower.

"What are we doing this weekend?" She asks as I lazily stroke the smooth expanse of skin. Her back is bare, the sheet piled at her narrow waist, covering her round globes that I so fondly enjoy palming as she lies on her tummy staring up at me. Violet gazes at me as if I'm the most interesting thing in the room, if only that were true. If only I could be quite so oblivious as she is, rather I'm jealously pondering ways of keeping her from my brothers. They're supposed to be the ones protecting her while I run the Vendetti Empire. Greedily, I can't stop from attempting to figure out ways to have her by my side at all times. Romano said it's my right to be selfish; I'm the head of the familia after all, even if it goes against my usual nature when mia familia is involved.

"You will be with me, of course." It comes out rougher than necessary with my tormented thoughts, imagining my wife naked and being fucked raw by Valentino or Dante. I know it would be either of them to consume her attention. *Am I enough for her, or will she run to one of their beds the moment she doesn't feel completely satisfied? I'm the Capo, much more powerful than any of them, she melts for my cock. I have to stop this frivolous jealousy. She belongs to me, not another; I own her in life and death.*

"That's not what I meant..." she trails off, innocent, eyes wide with surprise at my stiffening muscles. "I imagined we would be together."

I don't let her finish, raising an eyebrow, and staring down my nose into her irises, "Did you now? What else were you imagining, mia moglie?" The retort leaves me before I have time to think about what I'm saying. The lash striking out at her confidence like a painful whip wielded by none other than my controlling hand.

"Hey!" With an irritated huff, she rises onto her knees, pulling the sheet to cover her perfect breasts. "Why are you angry? You were inside me mere moments ago, whispering how wonderful I felt." With her brow scrunched in confusion, I can't help but feed off the sickly jealous thoughts infiltrating and poisoning my mind.

"So young and naive," My nostrils flare, smelling her sweet scent still lingering in the air. I had her screaming while she came around my cock, she's right, she did feel fucking fantastic. In fact, it's her fault for winding me up, making me feel such rapture and then having the plague of knowledge, knowing she'll be with a brother of mine sometime soon and also being aware that I can do absolutely nothing to put a stop to it.

Is it really the Vendetti tradition, or is it the Vendetti curse?

"Oh really...I'm young and dumb now, huh? Well, you're old and a dick." She remarks with a careless shrug, pulling the sheet a bit more to wrap around her to stand. She's so damn mouthy, and towards me of all people. If I were a lesser man I'd have her gagged for such disrespect. I should, just to prove a point to her that I can, I can do whatever the hell I want and she needs to remember that. Being mia moglie doesn't excuse her of being disciplined should the need arise.

"Where are you going?" I push, egging on an unnecessary argument. Watching her attempt to get away from me even quicker has my Vendetti temper flaring. The Capo rears his ugly head at not having his whim met immediately. Ruthless silently pounds at my temple to take what's rightfully mine, to break her down to submit. I'm her husband, me...not any of my brothers, nor any other man.

"I'm not laying here while you decide to talk down to me after I gave my body to you freely."

"Who will you run off to next, then?"

"You're unbelievable!" She scoffs and I rip the sheet out of her hands, wanting to hold her body to mine. Rather, she lets it go and practically hops away. I want to wrap her back up, shield her from others sight and lock her in here. If she won't outright obey, I'll wait her out, keep her only for myself.

The growl rumbles free, as I toss the vacated sheet off to the side. "You're not going anywhere," I command, on the cusp of raising my voice. It's so unlike myself, I feel as if I'm spiraling...I don't raise my voice, I don't ruffle, or even give a fuck. I demand, I take, I conquer- I claim what's mine. She's pushing me and it's dangerous, for her and for me. Violet's going to shove me too far and I'm going to lose control, something I didn't want to happen when it comes to her. To give in, is to surrender my control to her and I refuse to do so.

"I'm not staying here," she mutters yanking a t-shirt and shorts on. She leaves off the bra and the sight of her stiffened nipples underneath the thin material has me roaring.

"You will do as I say! I'm the capo dei capi Vendetti, damn it!" I move to grab her and she jerks away, anger pulling her lips tight.

"Make no mistake Matteo Vendetti, I'm more than aware of who you are. You seem to forget that you're also my husband." With a defiant huff, she spins on her heels and storms out of the room.

Full of frustration, my arm lashes out, making contact with a crystal vase. It flies to the floor, the loud shatter an echo of my loss of control over myself and of her. The bedroom door swings open in a flash, banging into the wall and an anxious Santino pops his head in, eyes wild.

"What the fuck is happening, Matty?"

"Nothing," the short reply leaves me with a curse. I could trash this entire room right now in a fit of fury. I'm so angry at her...fuck! I'm more furious with myself.

"I saw Vi, she took off down the hall as if she were being chased. Please tell me she's running after sex toys and not because you did something to upset her."

My glower seeks him out, "Her name's Vi-O-let, goddamn it. It's not Vi, not Bella, or any other fucking pet name!"

His hands shoot up, palms out, his mouth dropping at my outburst. "Calmati, Capo, per favore."

"Don't tell me to calm down. Mia moglie just ran down the hall, who is keeping her safe?" I shout, ready to lose it all over again and at someone who least deserves it. Not that Violet did, if anything I deserve to be on the receiving end of a lashing, tongue or whip.

He exhales, "Valentino ran after her. He'll make sure no harm comes to your wife. Do you want to tell me what's going on? What just happened?" He's shocked, they rarely witness me lose it like this, shaking and cursing like and addict. I'm not weak! Yet that woman has me between wanting to rage for her or bend to my knees and promise her anything her heart desires. Too bad for her, I'm not the type to bend.

Violet

I'm out the door in an angry flash, tired of his obnoxious mood swings. Storming down the hallway, I have no idea where I'm headed. In the moment I couldn't bring myself to care. I just need away from *him*. Why in the hell do I care so much? He's nothing but a stubborn, pig-headed Capo dei capi. I offer myself to him, open up, and tear down my walls, and he's selfish and rude in return.

Men confuse and anger me. I'm here away from my family, away from anyone I know, and he pulls this tantrum. I wish I could call my cousins and scream my frustrations out, but I can't. I'm married to the most powerful man around. I can't tell a soul about my grievances. That'll be the quickest method to getting my tongue removed. This is the mafia, I need to pull my big girl panties on and deal with it. Well, if I were wearing any.

Matteo's cum drips down my thighs, reminding me that he'd made love to me just before the awful remarks left his lips, angering me at him further. How dare he? I'm not some mistress he can cast aside when he feels broody. I'm his wife, damn it! I'm a Bottaro— was. I was a Bottaro. I'm a Vendetti now; he needs to remember that.

A quick hand grabs my bicep and I'm being spun around before I can take another step. I'm backed into the hallway wall with a large male body looming over me. Drawing in a deep breath with the impact, I catch the lingering scent of expensive cologne. It's the kind that makes me go dreamy inside, and instantly know it's Valentino's massive frame pressing into mine. The hallway's dark, with only a few dim sconces peppered about to illuminate the long corridor of what seems to be a never-ending mansion.

His nose goes to my neck, trailing upward to my hair as he scents me. He's a male in his prime with veins pumping full of powerful Vendetti blood. He's dangerous, just as Matteo— hell, as they all are— and overly intoxicating when it comes to my senses. "You being naughty, princess?"

I groan, already the wetness collecting between my thighs from mine and Matteo's morning bout of sex is mixing with my desire for Valentino. What have these men done to me? Making me into some sort of sex-starved woman, I want them all again and again. I shouldn't feel like this— crave all their cocks, especially the infuriating Capo. He wants to be vexatious and ask me about being with the others; well, I may as well do it. He doesn't care, after all, and he seems to enjoy pushing me toward them.

Valentino lifts me up, strong arms pulling and adjusting my thighs to each side of his hips as his erection grinds against my clit. It's enough pressure to have me seeing stars. With a pleased moan, my legs wrap around his hips. My ankles hook together over his muscular butt to hold him close as I mimic his previous move, grinding my core against his impressive length.

He grits his teeth, hot breath panting next to my ear, the fluttering making my nipples turn to stiff peaks. Valentino's sex personified. Dante may be my Casanova, Matteo my wild, moody beast, but Valentino is right there with them. To be fucked by the three of them at once would be more than I could ever handle, though a girl can dream. I'll tuck that fantasy away for a time when I'm not angry with any of them.

"You're running," he rasps, "and I enjoy chasing prey far, far too much for you to be able to handle."

"What do you do when you finally catch it?" I boldly question, and he growls with want or warning, I'm not certain.

"I conquer it," he shares, and I whimper. My cravings can't be natural. How can these crazy men get me so turned on? He takes a few steps to the side, keeping me seated to him. Fumbling with a knob, he gets it to twist, and then I'm being carried into a bedroom.

"Where are we?"

"Guest room," he answers. "Look at you. I told you not to leave that room unless you were dressed like a lady."

My lashes flutter. "You like me in pencil skirts and blouses so thin you can see my nipples in?"

"Undress, now," he orders with cheeks flushed. He stares at me, gaze full of pent-up desire. I think it turns him on even more when I don't follow the few basic rules he set about.

Yanking the shirt free, I toss it to the side then pull the shorts down that I'd hastily thrown on in my quick exit.

"No bra or panties?" he comments, irises flicking over every inch of exposed flesh. "Your slit leaks milky cream over those perfect pale thighs, and I swear I've never seen a woman look so fucking sexy. Except for when you were strapped to a table," he finishes on a growl, jerking his tie free. He carefully lays it on the bed, undoes each shirt button with quick, skilled fingers, then places his jacket and shirt neatly on the bed. He doesn't want a wrinkle in any item; so much like his asshole older brother. You'd think it'd be off-putting, when in reality it winds me up more. He pops the snap on his slacks, pushing them down, exposing his dark-blue briefs; the man has thighs so muscular I want to lick them. He toes expensive leather shoes off and lays the remaining clothing on the bed.

Stark naked, his long, hard, heavy cock shoots out toward me, eager for attention. His nostrils flair as he peers down at me. My chest heaves at his intense attention, his gaze watching as my breasts move. "Get in the shower. You're a dirty girl who misbehaves and you need to be fucked."

Valentino's sexy talk mixed with how turned on he is has me skittering toward the open bathroom door. He's right behind me, true to his word about enjoying the chase. It's intimidating, almost making me squeal with excitement. Stopping at the huge glass, walk-in shower, he reaches past me to flip the water on, and I swallow. I've never been fucked by Valentino without being restrained. I know he's rough and enjoys biting. Thankfully, I have some more experience so the thought doesn't terrify me but instead does the opposite.

His hand moves to the back of my hair, gripping it tightly. He can govern my movements, but it's not bad enough to cause me real pain. He likes control, as does my Matteo. Valentino's free hand caresses my bared flesh, a light graze over my breast, a careful caress over my abdomen. It's so at odds with his sharp, demanding ways that it has my head spinning and wetness pooling to drip down my thighs. His strong thumb trails over my ribs; it's a place I'd never imagined would be sensual. His touch moves to my back, the pressure massaging the tender muscle, then to my ass. His large palm cups the globe, as he leans in to trail his nose over my exposed shoulder. I'm nearly vibrating with the desire he's built up so quickly that I gasp when his teeth bite into my shoulder and two fingers enter my core from behind.

"Sopping wet, you dirty, dirty girl. Filled with cum and pussy juice, exactly how I enjoy it most. So fucking pink and pretty, princess. You ready to take my cock?"

"Yes." I swivel my hips, pushing my ass back toward him for more. My body shakes with desire, craving him to have his way with me.

He shoves me forward, and my body scrambles to keep up as his fingers are buried deep, and the other hand holds my head. He moves us into the shower, pressing my cheek against the cool glass. He leans in to whisper, "Careful, carina. I want to fuck that round ass you just offered, and big brother would be pissed if he didn't have it first."

His fingers leave my throbbing core, but the emptiness is swiftly replaced with the blunt head of his thick, hard cock. Fingers dripping with wetness are pushed into my ass, the whimper I'd held finally breaking free. His hips thrust, and my eyes clench closed. The sensations are riveting, his strong body so close, roughly pounding into me from behind. With one leg pushed farther up by his powerful thigh, he bends, driving upward repeatedly until I'm screaming for the release that's so damn close.

"Valentino!" I cry his name, ready to beg or plead for him to do whatever I need. My orgasm is just on the cusp. I need his filthy mouth to send me over. My hands against the steamy shower wall try to claw it, but I get nowhere as my fingers meet glass and not the flesh it craves to rip into. I want to slice up his back so later, when he sits down and leans back, he'll remember this, right now.

"Keep screaming my name. Let big brother hear how you enjoy my huge cock in that tight cunt. I'll fill you so full that my cum will leak out of your pussy all fucking day!" He pulls his fingers from my ass and smacks it hard enough that the sound echoes in the bathroom. Reaching around, his middle finger finds my clit, and one soft pat against it and I feel as if I'm airborne. My orgasm spirals through me, my mind flying with an intense burst of pleasure.

"Yes!" I scream and continue to spasm with the rewarding shocks. His cock pulses, hot cum bursting deep inside me as he roars out his release.

I guess that answered Matteo's question on who I'd fuck next, as he probably heard Valentino and I sounding like crazed animals going at each other. Do I feel guilty about it? Hell no. He's the one who shared them with me in the first place. Karma was him not expecting I'd enjoy it so damn much.

Matteo

Raking my hand through my sleep-flattened hair, a groan breaks free and I plant my ass on the bed in frustration. "Stupido," I mutter, shaking my head. "Era un argomento insulso che non aveva nessun senso."

"Really?" His brow lifts, surprised at my confession. "It's unlike you to argue for no reason, and for it to make no sense?" He tsks with disappointment.

"I was being jealous," I confess with an insolent shrug.

"Ah. You weren't expecting to like her and so fast?"

If it were any of my other brothers, I wouldn't be able to open up like this to them; I wouldn't feel comfortable confessing my screw up. It's rare that I do, ever. "Like isn't a strong enough word."

"She will be pregnant soon. How will you act when she is with child?"

"A wreck," I admit. I don't want to say it aloud, but the child better be mine. I'm a fool for believing I'd be okay with my brothers getting her pregnant. I know preserving the family bloodline is supposed to be the utmost importance, but I'm growing more and more territorial with Violet with each passing day.

"And what is your plan if we are supposed to be the one's keeping her safe all the time? You can't possibly keep her in your sights twenty-four hours a day. You have a business to run. An empire. Hell, the entire mafia practically."

"There's only one thing I can think of..."

He waits for me to say it, even though I know he's thinking the same thing I am.

"I have to make her a true queen. I have to teach her to run the Empire."

PART 2

THE VENDETTI *Queen*

CAPO DEI CAPI RUTHLESS
MATTEO VENDETTI

Santino shakes his head, fists clenching and unclenching before getting his bearings. "It's ludicrous. She's young and a woman. Vendetti women are the matriarchs of the familia, not the business. The Empire is for the men. You know this above any of us. It is our place to protect our women, not throw them into the ways of the mafia."

He's worried she'll be killed, and rightfully so. Women in our line of work rarely survive; they aren't hard enough to do the necessary evil it takes to remain on top. Being Romano's sons, we lack that issue and strive because of it.

Shrugging, I stand, grabbing my slacks that've remained neatly folded on the top of sofa at the end of the bed. Tugging them on and in place, I slip the clasp in the slot and meet my brother's gaze. "Then we'll teach her."

He turns away, muttering curses in Italian to himself. You couldn't have paid mia familia enough money to ever have them believing this would be my decision. It is, though, and it'll happen. Violet Vendetti will be not only my wife, but my queen. She'll learn to be a real Mafia queen, not only the matriarch of our familia, but the woman by my side while I head up the Vendetti Empire. And she'll be the first woman to ever hold such a place in mia familia's legacy.

Staring him down, aching for him to question me so I can unload some misplaced anger his way, I yank on my dress shirt. Snapping the platinum cufflinks in place, I quickly button the front neatly. Finally, he speaks.

"Please, Matty, you're sentencing her to death by doing this." It leaves him with a plea, but it's no use. My decision is final.

I've made up my mind and I'm not a man easily swayed. I don't bend— to anyone. "Then my brothers better get *fucking* off their minds and concentrate on her safety."

Chapter 1

"You are fierce. You're a survivor.
You're a fighter through and through.
Little brave, breathe.
There is a warrior within you."
-Beau Taplin

Matteo

A call comes in and immediately my gut clenches with knowing that Violet must've been contacted first. I never had my brothers take her phone back; it's being monitored. I should've, damn it.

"Cristiano, where is mia fiore?" He's been around me for the past few hours, but regardless, it's his duty to have an idea of where to find her. "You've all been warned to keep an eye on her throughout the day or night when she's not at my side. Who's with her right now?"

She's still salty over our fight too; I haven't spoken to her since this morning and wasn't planning to until dinner at eight. However, that doesn't mean I haven't periodically checked in with my brothers throughout the morning. My curiosity's gotten the best of me in regards to her temper and if she'd spoken to anyone about our argument. After that call, however, I cannot put off seeing her any longer.

"The last update I received said she'd locked herself in her bathroom and was sobbing while on the phone with someone. Before that, she was with Valentino most of the day." My brothers have taken to sending texts to each other so everyone always knows whether her safety is in jeopardy or if a break is needed.

"Fuck." The various important papers from my desk fly in multiple directions as my hand sails through the pile. I can't refrain from the burst of emotion having just been informed about what has my wife so upset. I keep losing control when it comes to her; it's making me unhinged. "Who's monitoring her phone line?" I should've been notified of the call the moment it came in.

"Sergio was put in charge of any incoming and outgoing calls, along with the wiretap we placed inside her bedside lamp. We have her monitored as you instructed. We'll know if there are any threats."

"The call I just received was informing me that the head of the Bottaro familia has been murdered."

"Shit..." he mutters. "Her father? The grandfather is long dead, no?"

"Si, and I'd bet my inheritance that the text you received about her wellbeing was because she somehow found out the news before me." A curse escapes as my hand fists. This isn't good at all. It has shady written all over it. I need to check on my wife. She's young and no doubt doesn't know how to deal with this. Violet's been far too sheltered growing up in this life only for her father to attempt to hide it from her.

"Do they have the killer?" He blows out a breath, pacing and texting someone rapidly. My guess would be he's informing our brothers on everything we're discussing.

"No. Text Dante and make sure he goes to her suite immediately." He'll peel the skin from any threat that attempts to get to her. He's one person I can trust that won't fuck up my orders and will protect her with his life.

"Violet will be safe here, Matteo. We have the best security in the state of New York. Hellhound Clinton herself couldn't weasel her way onto our property to tie up loose ends," he consoles, knowing where my thoughts are headed. If her father was murdered then the rest of her family will be next, I assume. Someone is on the hunt; they most likely want the familia out of the way to take their spot in Chicago.

A grunt leaves me as I stand. "It wouldn't surprise me if she was the one to take out the Bottaros in the first place," I mutter, having been well acquainted with how the politician takes care of her adversaries. She's tried to hire us in the past, with her being in New York.

"Wouldn't surprise me either," he smirks, falling in behind me as I swiftly make my way to the stairwell that'll lead me to the suite of rooms I'd given Violet upon coming to live with us. "You really care for this girl, no?"

We could take the elevator, I suppose, but I can run the steps of the staircase quicker than the elevator can get us there.

"She's no girl," I argue, flicking back a hard look at my youngest brother. The bastardo is nearly the same height and build as me already. In the end, he may surpass my frame, especially if he doesn't ease up on the gym time he's been obsessing about with Dante. "And, yes, of course I favor her. She's going to be the mother to my heirs someday, the queen to the Vendetti Empire. You should care as well."

"Are those the only reasons? Our brothers have been talking about you and her arguing. They have their own thoughts on how you may feel."

"Enough, Cristiano. My discussions with Violet are my business."

He quiets, doing as he's told, and continues to follow me until I reach my wife's door. I'm sure my flower is a mess, having already been told the news of her father's murder. We'll get through this and she'll grow stronger in the end.

"Don't interrupt unless I call for you."

"Yes, Capo." He nods as my waiting brothers tilt their heads in greeting. I repay them with the same acknowledgement, glad they didn't attempt to interrupt her. Inhaling a deep breath, I enter her room without bothering to knock. I own this damn house now; why the hell should I knock? Besides, she's my wife.

"Mia Violetta?" I call softly but loud enough she can hear me through the bathroom door. I have to remember to be consoling, to be soft. I'm not used to speaking to anyone this way, to comfort. I'll learn, though. I'll have her show me how to be decent at it. I'll have bambinos someday; I don't want them to believe me to be cold and unfeeling toward them.

Receiving no response, I lean in, placing my ear to the door. My breathing ceases as I attempt to hear a sniffle, a snore— hell, anything. I'm sure her heart is shattered at the moment, and while I was a bastardo to her earlier, I wish to bring her nothing but comfort in her time of grief. She will need me, and I'll be her strength through this.

"Mia bella moglie, please say something. Come, so I may hold you. I will protect you. We all will."

There's still no reply or any noise at all, and regardless of the melancholy she may be experiencing, I grow exasperated. With a twist of the decorative handle, I discover it's still locked as my brother mentioned earlier. "Violet, open the door, now." My patience is virtually nonexistent when it comes to this woman.

At the continued silence, my fist hits the door, echoing with the impact. My temper rears, and with a few rapid pounds, I expect her to shout or perhaps wake if she'd fallen asleep. There's nothing yet again. With an impatient jerk, I end up ripping the stupido dainty handle from the door. I let out a curse and my body slams against the thin wood, the door easily flying inward with so little of my effort. I really need to get a better door put on in its place. God forbid it be someone else and not me trying to get to her next time. I have to keep her safety in mind always. I'd never forgive myself if she were harmed all because of a damn door.

I'm met with an empty room and a cracked window. I thought her room felt cooler when I came in, but I was too focused on getting to her to give it any real thought. Each set of suites has its own thermostat for individual comfort as well. If one of us wanted it to be fifty degrees in our room, it could be and no one would know any different in their own space. A luxury that has quickly become a hindrance as my brothers would've felt the coolness in the hallway and known something was amiss.

"Violet?" I utter, although there's no one there.

I already know what to expect when I rush to the window and shout for my brothers to join me. There's no sign of her below, just snowless lattice where she appears to have climbed down from her bathroom window and sloppy footsteps leading off into the yard. If it weren't for the thin layer of snow having fallen earlier this evening, I'd have no idea which direction she'd gone or if she were alone in the endeavor. Thankfully, there is only one set of prints leading off into the dark. Unfortunately, that also means she's out there with no protection.

"Capo?"

"Matty?"

My brothers all echo as they pile in around me, gazing out the overly large window to see what I'm staring at.

"Is she?" Luciano begins, and I nod. I don't need to hear him say it out loud. This is a huge screw up, one that never should've happened in this household.

I'm so enraged at the moment but must keep my wits about me. I have to be calm because she's my priority. "We must find her. She's upset, her father's dead, and there's a killer on the loose hunting Bottaros. I'd seen the threats the night of the wedding. Romano showed me as we'd waited for the doctor to look her over. The demands were juvenile in nature compared to what we've dealt with in the past towards our familia. They'd called for her severed head, but I was certain the union between her and I would put a stop to the Bottaro threat for the most part."

"Do we know who it could be?" Salvatore steps closer, grumbling under his breath about Violet catching pneumonia out there. The last thing I need to be thinking about is her being cold and getting sick. I'm already worried immensely about her ending up with her throat slashed. Pneumonia can be cured. Death...not so much.

"I want to know how in the fuck she got outside without the alarms and where she is right this minute. Alarms should've been triggered; the house speakers should be shrilling in warning this very minute. You all brag about the top-of-the-line security, yet my young wife just gave you guys the slip and we have no idea where she could be! How in the hell does one woman evade seven Vendettis, guards, and a sensitive alarm system?" My voice finishes nearly yelling in my anger as I glare at my brothers. They silently glower at the marble floor, taking my fury with their dutiful submission. Of course they have nothing to say in return. A group of dangerous, intelligent men acting like a bunch of ten-year-old shmucks whose balls haven't dropped yet.

Valentino finally speaks, as I'm about to blow a gasket. "I've alerted the men. I have Angelo and Luigi searching the grounds. Severo is scanning the cameras and Vito has pulled up the GPS locator apps in case she takes a car. We'll find her, Capo."

While I was furiously staring out the open bathroom window, he was busy. I'm glad that one of them has their head in the game. The rest? Well, if I were my father, I'd be planning out punishments already. I'm not writing it off just yet either. If they don't bring me my wife and in one, healthy piece, they will hurt for it.

"We better. *I swear to Christ* she better be alive and well whenever we do, too, or else you all will be punished for this. She's the future of this family, for fuck's sake. Violetta could already have my heir growing in her belly. I want her safe; locked in this fucking house, where she belongs."

"We'll find her, Matty," Salvatore echoes, and I growl, storming out of the bathroom.

Snatching her coat from a chair as I go, my brothers nearly run to keep up with my brutal pace. I don't give two shits if they've notified the guards. If I want something done, I guess I need to do it myself. Just as I knew I needed to be the one to keep an eye on her, and I was right. One small argument and now she's gone and possibly in danger. I never should've lost control of my jealousy. My possessiveness pushed her away. Had I not been so stubborn this morning, then most likely she would've been in my office pestering me when that call came through.

"Damn gullible woman." Grumbling, I jerk on my wool jacket. Pulling it over my wide shoulders, I yank out my phone.

Thankfully, my wife's wedding ring has a tracking device set under the massive-sized diamond. The jeweler was smart enough to make the color match with the platinum back so you can't notice it when looking directly at the stone. My father was always one to be prepared. I believed I was the same, but after this, it's apparent I need to step it up a few notches.

My hand pats my pocket, finding my keys where I'd left them, thankfully. "I'll turn my locator app on so I can track her ring. It'll sync the directions to my Range Rover. Someone follow me in a car in case we need to chase her down. Any news on what vehicle she's taken?" There's no way she'd stay on foot; she's far too smart for that.

Cristiano jogs up beside me. "Vito said a BMW was gone."

"Which model?" I huff, tearing through the mansion to get to the garage.

"It was a three."

"Good, then she won't be able to go too fast in it, unless it was one of your specialty models?" My father has a habit of giving us fast cars for Christmas and our birthdays. We have a garage full of at least thirty gifted vehicles. It's a bit atrocious, if I'm being honest about it. Apparently, in his lack of parenting, he believed luxury vehicles would make up for it.

"No, it was one of the cars the staff uses."

"Keep me updated," I demand as I finally make it to my blacked-out Range Rover. Valentino and Dante head for a Lamborghini, while Luciano and Santino jump into my vehicle. My gaze flicks to Cristiano and Salvatore. "I want you both here in case you hear something or she comes back for some reason. We need to be spread out so one of us can get to her immediately."

Normally, they'd be the first two to argue, but they must notice the unwavering determination reflected in my gaze as they simply nod and wish us a safe and quick recovery. I only hope when I get to mia Violetta that she's not hurt and I can stop her from being the next victim. I've merely gotten her in my life; I don't want to lose her already.

And so help any person that lays a finger on her. It'll be their death.

Chapter 2

Her courage was her crown

and she wore it like a queen.

-Atticus

Violet

I'm actually driving! I haven't ever driven a car like this. My father never wanted myself or my mother to learn how to drive; he thought there was no reason when we had a car and driver to take us everywhere. The head of his security insisted that, for our safety, every family member had to learn. I took the written test and drove around a parking lot in a fancy Mercedes for a private driving test and got my license. I wasn't worried at the time, believing my father's insistence that I'd never have to use it, but I'm thankful for it now.

I have to get home, right now. There's no way my husband would let me leave, nor would any of his brothers, no matter how much I tried to beg any of them. So rather than waste time I don't have, I scaled the fence and took a car as soon as I found one. I'm Matteo's wife; I'm technically a Vendetti now, so they can't get too angry at me for borrowing a car. It was on the property with the key fob thing in it, so it must be one of the brother's.

My head is scattered with worry and heartbreak. I can focus on nothing but getting home this very moment. Thankfully, all these nice cars do the work for you. I typed in my family's address and it brought up the directions I needed to find my way back. Now, I have to make it in one piece without wrecking.

I want to fly down the street, but it's winter and roads are icy. I remember the study guide said to drive ten under the speed limit in imposing weather, but other people are driving like maniacs. Maybe it's New York, or just because I'm new at this? The speed limit says fifty-five and I'm carefully going ten under, yet they pass me so quickly. I wish I'd had practice at driving, I hate not being prepared. I don't have a choice though.

My mother will be killed next, if I don't make it back in the allotted time. The directions given were simple: pull myself together and get to my family's house by tomorrow. I'm supposed to come alone, if I want my mother to have any chance to survive. I don't doubt the threat for a moment either. I can't believe this is happening. The whole point of me marrying Matteo was so this wouldn't be an issue any longer. The death threats were supposed to disappear or at least fade away, according to my father. My poor papa...I'm so sad he's dead. Though I can't focus on my grief right now. I need to concentrate on driving.

I have to take Matteo's advice and be strong. Who'd have thought that my husband's rude comments would come to use so quickly after he'd made them. Of course, I'd sobbed during the phone call. Who wouldn't have? I'd just been informed that my father was brutally murdered and that my mother would be next...that I could possibly save her. From that point, I was on autopilot. I climbed out a freaking window, into the freezing wintery night, and took a car! My father was right to tell me that I'm a bit reckless; I can see his meaning now.

Hmm, me reckless and Matteo's ruthless. What a fitting combination.

Tears fall down my cheeks, but I pay them no mind. With a quick swipe here and there, I stare ahead out the front window. My back's straight and my nerves are wrung tight, not wanting to screw this up and get pulled over. I know Matteo has plenty of the cops in his pocket; he's the Capo. You don't get to that station without having plenty of people to call when you want something. One wrong swerve and a cop could notice me, returning me to my husband before I have a chance to even leave the city. I won't be quite as worried once I'm farther out and his reach is less and less. It's not that I'm frightened of him...Okay, so I am. But that's not why I'm fearful of getting stopped by an officer. It's because I know Matteo wouldn't allow me to go. I must evade him as much as possible so I can get to my mother.

More tears fall; I sniff and wipe my face. My thoughts play over the last conversation I had with my papa. I was so damn angry with him, but thankfully I wasn't too stubborn to tell him that I love him. I would feel much worse about that conversation had I not said it. He was such a kind man to me, always. I was not an easy daughter, and being a Princessa of a Chicago mob family, it was almost expected of me. I wanted my way when I wanted it. He was always patient with me through the constant picking my mother did; she'd swear I would never marry well with my terrible mannerisms. He didn't believe that, and I will miss him.

No matter what my mother and I have been through with our rocky relationship, I can't let her die. I would never forgive myself. I have a chance to put a stop to it, so I must. I know I promised my loyalty to Matteo, and I meant it, but she's still my mother. I have to at least attempt to help or else I'll be worse than she ever was with her snide comments and underhanded ways. There's a piece of me that wonders if the roles were reversed, would she do the same for me? Of course she would. I'm her daughter, in the end. At least, I hope she would.

Loud honking shakes me out of my thoughts. Blinking, I jerk to the left, realizing I was halfway into the other lane. A red light appears on the dash with a chime. The GPS alerts me that it's searching for nearby gas stations.

"I didn't ask you to search for a gas station!" I yell, full of frustration. I need to get home, not refill the tank. I don't know how to fill the freaking car up anyhow. Surely, they must have some places that fill the tank for you? Besides, I don't have money with me... Maybe there's a credit card stored somewhere in here.

With a groan, I grab the air freshener from the vent and fling it into the passenger window. "I need to get to my family, damn it!" Another honk warns me that my tantrum has me swerving again, and I jerk into my lane then let go, screaming as the GPS repeats that she's rerouting.

I feel helpless and I absolutely can't stand it. I'm strong, damn it. I know I am! My father was just murdered, but I'm going to keep it together to help my mother. I silently chant to myself as my sobs grow heavier. I'm a fucking mess.

"This is your fault, papa!" I spew as the tears continue to fall. I drive until the car chimes several times and begins to almost cut off. I have a feeling I've broken it by not taking it to a gas station as it instructed. I couldn't help it though; I need to get home as quickly as possible. I can't stop for gas. This is a small car; can't it drive for a while?

It sputters again, losing speed. The dash flickers an angry red E at me and people are speeding by with various honks. Of course this would happen right now. The woman, who doesn't drive, ends up taking the car that runs out of gas. I'm so angry and overwhelmed, I could punch something. Not that it would do me any good. It's fucking freezing outside and I'm on the side of the road with no heat. The car ran out of gas, my father was murdered earlier, my mother is next to die, and I was fighting with my husband the last time we spoke. Could this night get any worse? I'm scared to even ponder the thought.

Reciting prayers has done nothing. I keep praying, waiting for the Almighty to come to my rescue. Where's the do-gooder stopping by with fuel or offering me a safe ride? I need help, and at my lowest, I need a sense of newfound hope.

I do what any young, inexperienced woman my age would do: I sit in the car that swiftly grows cold and cry my eyes out. So much for being strong right now. I feel like a complete fool at the moment. I have to find someone to help me, but who? My cousins can't do a thing with me out here. Sure, one could send a car, but that would take forever to get here, and by the time I made it to my family's home, I'd be too late. I can't call my mother, and if I call Matteo, he'll bring me back to the estate. I'll be locked away with increased security and never be able to reach my mother or anyone for that matter. She'll be killed and laid with my already-deceased father.

Tossing my useless phone on the passenger seat, I climb out of the vehicle. Cars zip past me, the icy wind bites into my skin, and the tears fall with a flourish. I'm useless, always having to depend on others. When this is all over, I need to have a serious chat with the Capo. He has to be open in giving me some sort of independence so I can survive on my own if I ever need to. I know his brothers would be there for me, but in a situation such as this, it's all useless. They wouldn't help me get to my mother right now; they'd do Matteo's bidding and have me locked in my room as quickly as possible.

I'm reduced to begging from a Good Samaritan. Standing behind the small BMW, I wave my hands at the many cars zipping past me. They pay me no mind, besides a few random honks here and there. Not that I can blame them; it's dark and I'm looking like a hot mess.

They probably think I'm nuts, not that I need a ride to help save my mother.

Finally, after who knows how long, a sleek-looking sports car pulls over. My arms are frozen as I stop my frantic waving. Hell, my entire body feels frozen. Hopefully, whoever this is, they don't recognize me as the Capo's wife. Surely, very few people in New York actually know what I even look like. The passenger door opens, the interior light illuminating a big man.

He stands and closes the door, turning in my direction. It registers who he is and a gasp leaves me.

Dante Vendetti. Shit.

His eyes are wide, crazed even as he approaches me with angry steps. "Do you have any idea how fucking stupido this was of you? How dangerous?"

I'm shaking so badly that his anger morphs to concern and he yanks me to his huge, hulking body. Muscles and warmth crush me to his frame as he furiously grumbles, "It's fucking freezing and anyone could've gotten you." His hands move up and down my body, bringing warmth into my limbs, blocking the chilling wind.

His comfort has me shaking more, relief and exhaustion setting in. His voice, his heat...it's everything I needed right now and didn't realize it. "Dante," I breathe into his wide chest. "I need you."

Then his hands are moving, cupping my face, tilting it up to his. His lips fall to mine in a sweltering kiss, bringing life back to the frozen feature, and I can't seem to get close enough to him as I crawl up his body. He embraces me, his kiss punishing as he ravages my mouth. I'm no longer cold as a burning ember blossoms in my core, heating me from inside.

Pulling away, I admit again against his mouth, "I need you, Dante, so badly."

With a growl, he lays me over the tiny iced-up trunk of the car and yanks my yoga pants down my thighs. With a few shifting movements, he pushes my thighs together over one of his arms and then is thrusting into me deeply. His free hand comes to rest around my throat.

"I should choke the fucking life from you for pulling this shit. You had us raging with worry," Dante utters with a grunt and thrusts hard enough to drive my body into the cold metal. "Matteo will be absolutely furious. You will be punished!" Another powerful plunge into my heat and I'm moaning so loudly I must sound like a dying cow.

"P-please, Dante." I don't even know when the begging began, but I need him to give me a twisted sense of the normalcy I've come to expect in my time being a Vendetti.

His hand squeezes my neck tight enough to have me seeing spots, and then I'm coming all over his thick cock. "Yes, oh God, yes!" I scream, and with a hard drive, he's filling me with his seed. It's hot and slippery and everything I needed in the moment.

Dante pulls free, the cold instantly hitting my thighs, and I shiver. A new batch of goose bumps covers my skin as he tucks his length back into his pants. He moves, pulling my thin black yoga pants in place, then helps me off the vehicle, cocooning me in his bulk. As he turns toward the awaiting vehicle, he's met with a fist. The crack's loud enough it has me wincing and ducking free.

My husband has arrived and Dante was right...he's not happy.

"Fuck!" Dante shouts as the hit settles in. His fists clenched, breaths coming heavily, puffs of white smoke fill the air in front of us. His jaw clenches, teeth gritting together as he stares down his older, violent brother.

"I told you to find her, not fuck her," Matteo warns, then grabs my bicep, yanking me to him. In an instant, my coat is wrapped over my shoulders and I'm being carried princess-style to an awaiting SUV.

"Matteo, please, I'm sorry."

His harsh glare cuts to me, leaving his brother in our wake. With powerful strides, we're at the SUV in no time, the back door being held open by a worried looking Santino. He casts me a gaze full of pity as Matteo loads us into the back. He puts me on his lap and barks, "Drive!" to Santino.

The heat's turned up, blowing plenty of hot air to the back, stinging my skin. "Matteo, please," I mutter, not above groveling. He has to understand I have an important reason for taking off like I did. The vehicle pulls out, gravel and snow flying as we lurch back onto the busy road. The sports car follows closely behind, and they drive far faster than I ever could've attempted.

"Begging will get you nowhere with me, carina. You will find I punish those around me for less."

A tear works its way free, cascading over my cheek. I've been a blubbering mess since I found out my father was murdered. I don't have time to stop and grieve right now, so I have to do it this way, I suppose. "My father was killed," I choke the words out, swallowing a few times as to not wretch with the severity of their meaning.

He nods, his gaze not quite as harsh with my vulnerable admission.

"M-my mother is next."

He nods again. "I know. Who do you think is on that list afterwards? And you're out running free with no protection. Tell me, mia moglie, how long do you think it would've taken until someone found you on the side of the road? They would've loved having you like that, so defenseless. An easy picking for a chump, so foolish," he scoffs, and my face heats in embarrassment.

"Please don't do that...not right now."

"Do what?" he mutters, tucking his arms around me. I couldn't move from his lap if I wanted anyhow. I already know that much.

"Don't scold me as if I'm a stupid child. I left because my mother's being threatened, and the caller told me I could possibly save her if I got home in time."

He sighs, his eyes clenching closed for a moment as he collects himself. "Your father, God rest his soul, was an idiot for leaving you so innocent. It's more dangerous than endearing."

Another tear falls and I hastily swipe it away. No matter if my papa is gone or not, I don't like crying in front of Matteo for any reason. He pulls me closer into his body and tucks my head under his chin. With a sniffle, I pull myself together enough to bring up what I admitted a moment before.

"I have to go to her, Matteo. I need to try to save her. I'm the only hope she has."

"There's no way you can save her. This is exactly why your father gave you to me. He knew that it was only a matter of time before he died the same with the rest of his familia."

"You're powerful, you're the Capo. Please h-help me."

He tsks. "And what, mia Violetta? You expect me to load my brothers up, order my men along so we can go and clean house in a city that I'm not even in charge of? You would risk all their lives for one old woman who treated you so poorly? I think not."

"I don't expect you to risk anyone. I will kill the person responsible for this. They would never expect it."

"You?" He chuckles, amusement laced in his voice. "You can't even drive a car without it running out of gas."

Chapter 3

"She was brave and strong

and broken all at once."

- Ana Funder

"If you recall, I was able to take that car in the first place," I remind him, and his chest stops shaking with laughter.

"It was reckless," he hisses, and I shrug.

"I'll do it again, if I have to, if you won't help me."

With a growl, he squeezes me tight enough I nearly squeak. "Don't threaten me. I can easily tie you up and you won't be able to move a limb unless I deem it." He's such an entitled jerk, and damn it, he smells amazing, which makes it even worse. How I can be attracted to him at a time like this is beyond me.

Clearing my throat, I hedge, "You want me to have your children." I bring up the one subject I know he's extremely passionate about, looking to bargain. I have to get him on board somehow, and at this rate, I'll do whatever it takes.

"Si." He nods, his chin moving against the top of my head. "You will have mia bambino soon, fiore."

Matteo Vendetti is so sure when he speaks, like it's already set in stone. Yet, I persist. It's not in me to give up when I want something.

"If you take me to my family's home by tomorrow, I'll willingly have ten of your children. I'll do whatever you want me to, to be your dutiful wife. No more fighting from me, Matteo. I just need you to give me this."

"You're striking a deal with me?" He sounds skeptical and a bit shocked, but of course he is. He believes I hold no pull in this, that I have nothing to bargain with, but he's wrong.

"Yes, I'm not above bartering for what I want." My papa told me to always have a plan. A good talker can be the difference between life and death at times. The current situation being my mother's life, not mine.

His head shakes. "You do have a spine, mia moglie, I'll give you that. It may be buried deep, but it's in there." I don't know what he means by that, and I don't ask. "Say I'm willing to come to a... agreement of sorts. You'll do anything? No matter what I request of you?"

"*After*," I emphasize, "we go to my family's home. By tomorrow, *and* you help me kill my father's murderer. I will do whatever you ask of me." I bite the inside of my bottom lip, waiting for him to speak. This is my one chance, I can feel it. The guy is stubborn, but he's also spoiled, and this is a way he gets what he wants from me willingly. I may regret this decision; in fact, I can almost bet money on it that I will. A cornered, desperate woman will do what she has to though.

"Killing them won't be the issue. Your safety is my top priority, however, and having you 'help' is what concerns me."

I'm shaking my head before he can finish. "Look at me, Matteo." I lean forward so he can take in my swollen eyes, my glossy lips, covered in the gloss's pink sparkles and minty scent. "I look anything but threatening. If anything they'll think I'm an easy target."

He scoffs, yanking me back to his warm, solid chest. "Because you are." I move to protest, but he cuts me off. "However, I understand your point, and we'll figure something out. As long as a few of my brothers and plenty of men are with us, it'll be hell for anyone to lay a hand on you."

"So you'll do it?" I breathe with my chest beginning to foolishly fill full of hope. I can't believe he's even considering it. I may need his help, but I know he'll no doubt be stubborn about the entire process. The Capo likes things done his way; his brothers have forewarned me already.

"Let's see if you're that excited once you hear the price."

I wish he wouldn't say that and allow me to pretend to be naïve, but it's not the case. He does come outright with the warning, and I'd already been feeling a bit suspicious. His voice rises as he speaks to his brothers in the front seats. "Santino, head for the jet. Luciano, text Dante. Have him and Valentino follow us. Also, Severo, Vito, Angelo, and Luigi need to know to meet us there as well. Tell Cristiano to alert the crew to have the jet on standby for us."

"We're flying?"

He grunts before threading his fingers into my hair and whispering into my throat, "We won't be walking, that's for certain. Besides, you have some groveling to do for taking that car, and the plane will be the perfect place to begin your first lesson on your knees."

Oh my.

I can feel his hardness under my thigh, but it seems he plans to act on it. Was it because he showed up witnessing Dante fucking me on the side of the road? "You didn't have to hit Dante."

A growl rumbles his chest, making him sound more lion than man. "The hell I didn't. He was fucking you."

"I told him I needed him. I was freezing," I admit on a whisper. I don't know why I get quiet speaking about it; he's seen them all between my thighs.

His fist tightens in my windblown locks. "You should stop speaking about him before we get to the jet."

"But why?" I can't help but blurt, my curiosity overpowering my common sense.

His nose scents my neck, his lips softly grazing as he mutters, "Because I said so. Because I want to fuck you. Because I'll hurt you in this small space. Because you need to be punished for your foolishness, and he was there, busily sinking his cock into my wife's pussy without my consent."

A shiver races over my flesh at his possessive proclamation. He nips my throat, reminding me of his brothers simultaneously biting me while I was being fucked in the exam room. A low moan leaves me as I squirm, pressing my legs together. I'm no longer scared of that room and what they planned to do to me. It was amazing; I've never come so many times before.

"You want that?" he utters into my flesh, his mouth creating delicious goose bumps with each pass of his lips. "You want me to fuck you in the backseat while my brothers try not to wreck from watching us? Does that sweet little cunt need my cock, mia Violetta?"

"Oh." With a sigh, my legs squeeze together again, only to be wrenched apart. He leaves my clothes on, but his hand at my back snakes around, three strong fingers covering my core. He rubs, side to side, until I'm panting, then switching he moves those fingers up and down. Matteo applies just enough pressure to have me moaning loudly, mad with desire. I'm right on the border, listening to him speak those dirty thoughts into my neck while grabbing my hair and now rubbing my pussy until my hips chase his movements. I'm eager and so damn needy whenever it comes to his touch.

"That drenched pussy needs to be filled. Such a shame, since you'll be on your knees sucking my dick until I allow you to swallow my cum." His hand switches it up again, moving in circles, and I lurch upward, the sensation exactly what I needed. Knowing he plans to punish me in the delightful way of sucking him off once we get to the plane, paired with his powerful touch, has me moaning again as my orgasm hits and pushes me further to the edge.

I'm teetering on a rocky ledge; I just need that tiny bit to throw me into bliss completely. It happens when his tongue licks up my neck, the air following along like a delightful wisp. My legs are spread as widely as possible in this position, my hips rotating, no shame whatsoever as Matteo strokes my yoga-covered pussy. One last moan and I shudder, my gaze flicking to catch Santino's in the rearview mirror. He's breathing heavily, his cheeks warm as he does his damndest to watch us in the backseat. He wants to be fucking me right now, I can see it. He wishes his cock was driving into me this very moment.

"Drive, Tino," Matteo orders, and then the watchful eyes in the mirror are gone as he concentrates on the road out the front window.

Sucking in a breath, my gaze momentarily moves to the right, finding Luciano just as flushed as Santino had appeared. They were staring, witnessing me come before them. Matteo was right, they would've easily wrecked the vehicle had my husband stripped me bare and fucked me the way he no doubt desires. What's it going to be like on the jet? Hopefully, there's at least a partition from the pilot. Not that I'm worried about him taking me in front of his brothers; he's already done that. In fact, I think I'd enjoy it even more than I had the first time around. Now, I know they'll take care of me and make me feel good— not much to complain about in that department.

My husband's hand comes to my chin, tipping it upward. Turning my face, I meet his gaze. "Say thank you," he orders, and I nearly sputter.

"Ex-excuse me?"

"I allowed you to come after you defied me by jeopardizing your safety. If I were a harder man, I'd have held it back, watched you uncomfortable."

I snort, I can't help it. "You, harder? First of all, you're the biggest badass of a man I've ever met, and secondly, you're quite solid under my thigh." I throw in a wink for good measure and his lips twitch. He wants to be pissed, but I'm making it difficult for him, and thankfully he's proving to be an excellent distraction from my stressful evening.

His gaze grows stern, and after a moment, I remember the deal I'd been attempting to strike with him. He's taking me to the airport, so I nod. "Thank you," I swallow, not allowing my pride to get in the way.

"Good," he comments, and then his lips are on mine. The kiss is full of ownership and dominance. I merely came moments ago, and yet the twist and turn of his tongue has me hot and needy all over again. How do these Vendettis get me like this? I'd never even had sex before coming to the estate, and now I can't seem to get my fill of it.

The drive isn't too long, but it certainly seems so as my anxiety eats away at my nerves. Matteo is good at distracting me, but it's not enough to chase the reality away completely. I'm wrecked inside that my father is dead, but I can't let myself break down like my mind wants me to. I have to get to my mother; I need to see my family and try to help them. I never would've believed that Matteo would come to my aid in this whole plan of mine. It certainly helps that he's a mob boss and has various resources right at his disposal.

We arrive at the private airport strip and his jet is nothing to scoff at. It speaks of just how much wealth his family has. We've flown privately quite often, but this is his actual jet. As in, his family owns it. That's next level compared to what I'm used to. Not that it matters to me, but I'm grateful for it in this circumstance.

"Do you need anything before we depart?" Valentino checks with Matteo and me as I get my seat belt secured in place. Some of his men were waiting for us when we arrived, ready to load up. I noticed they had a variety of bags with them as well. I wonder what they're filled with. I doubt it's all designer suits for the Vendettis. Probably a small arsenal of weapons to help with this little endeavor of ours.

I shake my head, as does Matteo, and Valentino takes the seat behind ours, Dante's across the tiny walkway, and the others are off farther toward the back.

The bossy male leans in to murmur, reminding me of his earlier demands of having me on my knees, "We'll go to the bedroom once we're in the air."

My gaze meets his. Matteo's irises are still swirling, full of pent-up desire. "There's a bedroom on here?" I ask naïvely, and he chuckles.

"There's an office, large bathroom, and bedroom with a queen-sized bed, along with a small kitchenette for drinks and snacks." He grins, and it reminds me of a wolf about to prance. "Also a smaller bathroom as we entered the plane."

"Did you decide yet what you wanted in return for all of this?" I finally ask. It's been playing on my mind ever since we struck the initial agreement. He's Matteo Vendetti, the Ruthless Capo dei capi...The man doesn't need to bargain with anyone. He simply snaps his fingers and those around him jump or else end up buried. The concept's simple, really.

"I knew what I wanted from the moment you struck the deal with me. I always have something planned prior to agreeing to anything of the sort. You should not undermine your opponent."

"I thought you're my husband, not an opponent."

"I am, mia fiore, but in that moment you were striking a bargain not as my wife. You did not come to me and ask for my help as my bride. You said you'd be willing to risk anything, even give me children if I wanted. That's a plea from a helpless woman. It was never a request from the Capo's wife, from the queen."

"You confuse me, speaking in circles. You want me strong yet patronize me when I take a car and attempt to drive myself. Yet when I ask for help, you make me sound like someone off the street looking for a loan."

He tsks, "You taking a car doesn't make you strong; it makes you reckless. You were being careless with your life and the future of our bloodline. Actions as such won't impress me; they infuriate me."

I release a huff as he continues his tirade.

"You want to be the Vendetti queen, carina? You want to earn my respect? Then fucking act like it. You tell me what you need, you call in the jet then you alert the men. You come up with a plan and stand straight while you do the entire thing. That is what a queen does, little Bottaro princessa. You want so much, yet have you truly stood up and taken your place to request such things? You bargain with me over my future sons, yet don't expect to be treated as if I'm a loan shark. The Vendetti queen wants the sons as badly as I do because it helps secure her future as well as my own." His rant finally comes to a stop on an irritated hiss.

I suppose I should be worried about him showing emotion that's outside of the bedroom or not teasing and getting him wound up enough to lecture me. Is this what Santino was warning me about? He told me I won't like Ruthless, and I promised that I wasn't here to rock the boat, yet my husband sugar coats nothing when it comes down to it. I suppose I should be grateful he's willing to lay it out a bit for me. I feel every bit of my nineteen years old when he speaks to me in such a way, though, and that I definitely don't care for.

I want him to see me as an equal, as his wife, and yes, respect me. I never would've just paused in the middle of my panic to let everyone know what I needed. I would've pleaded or thrown a tantrum. He's right, I'm supposed to sit at his side and I need to start acting like it. I've automatically expected him to hand me everything since I've arrived. It's time that *I* treat him as *my* equal.

Chapter 4

She's a combination of sensitive and savage.

-Quotes 'nd Notes

Matteo

The plane levels out and I get to my feet, gesturing for Violet to do the same. She owes me, and it's time I collect. Clasping her wrist in my palm, I lead her toward the back of the plane, pointing out the area for drinks and snacks, then continue to show her the bathroom, office, and finally the bedroom. When I'd initially discovered she was gone from the house, I straight out panicked inside. I'm not used to feeling such a thing. I'm always cool, calm, collected, and in control. My father instilled the emotions into me every single day of my life, but just the thought of her blood being spilled had me choking up inside.

I'd felt such relief when her location stopped moving on the ring locator app and I could pin her down. Thanks to that locater— the one I'd thought was a ridiculous idea before this happened— I knew she'd stayed with the vehicle too. The tracker was one of the best purchases I've made to date, and I'll be investing in more pieces with the same technology. After this, however, I may have a doctor shoot a tracker straight into her damn body. It'd be far too easy for some schmuck to steal her ring if she's ever without protection again. The woman is destined to give me an early heart attack if she's going to pull this again in the future.

The relief of discovering her location was short-lived, as I pulled my Range Rover to a stop. My headlights had only amplified the sight before me. They further illuminated the cars headlights to shine over Violet and Dante. My brother was fucking her with a punishing force, and it infuriated me to no end. Here I was speeding down the highway like a madman possessed, risking mine and my brothers' lives on the icy roads, while she was busy getting fucked by Dante. At that very moment, it took everything in me to rein in my anger, clench my fist, and strike Dante only once. What I'd actually wanted was to beat him so badly he couldn't walk, but that's not my place. It's not the Vendetti way, after all. I have to find a means to move past this possessiveness in me when it comes to Violet and mia familia.

She has every right to be with my brothers should she choose. After the scare for her in danger, I'd thought I'd made peace with it too. I was foolish to believe her safety was everything and I'd gladly share her as long as she returned to me unharmed. I was stupido to have such foolish thoughts. Mia fiore is mine; she belongs to me. That's where this deal comes into play. She wanted to bargain? Well, she should be careful what she wishes for. I'll help her with this mindless request, then she'll have to honor what I have in store as payment. She shouldn't even be wasting her time with this, but who am I to stop her when it'll benefit me in the end. Her mother will end up dead regardless. It's just the way it is. The Bottaros weren't only enemies with my familia; they had others, and I'm assuming someone has come to collect their bodies.

Regardless, I'll humor Violet. I doubt her mother will still be breathing by the time we land. It is what it is. I won't be the one to break the news to her; rather, I'll use it to my advantage. The situation will afford me the optimal opportunity to swoop in and offer her support and tenderness. It'll push her one step closer to falling in love with me over everyone else.

Cunning? Yes, perhaps a bit. In the end, however, it brings me closer to what I desire. I didn't become the Capo— the top in the game, the head of The Vendetti Empire— by mistake. I'm the best at what I do. I am the mob, and I got here for a reason. I'm Ruthless and it would do Violet some good if she never forgets that.

"Remove your shirt," I order as she steps into the tiny bedroom. It fits a queen-sized bed, but there's not much room for anything else. Ever since I saw her with Dante, I've been gritting my teeth, wanting to sink into her and replace his cum with my own. The need to breed her is like an unwavering itch that I can't reach until I see her belly swell with my child. The fact that his cum was in her last is grating at me like a knife to the spine.

She quickly does as she's told, chest heaving, with her growing anticipation. She knows I'll be a little rough with her, understands that I crave her submission, that I need it. Now to teach mia fiore to be as strong as steal when required— that's the next step to putting her at the top.

Her thin sweater and jacket lie in a heap on the floor, and so help me, I want to chastise her for it. I could be an even bigger jerk and have her stop to fold it neatly; that's what my father would do in my place. I don't, but that little bit of restraint has me on edge. The sight of her pale, bared breasts pulls my attention away from the mess. She's so goddamn beautiful. Even after crying away the evening, she has me catching my breath as I stare my fill. Silver dollar-sized tan nipples beg me to suck and nip at them. If this was about her, I could make her come from only messing with those perfect breasts.

Out of all the women to be offered to me to wed, I was granted a piece of heaven and wasn't even aware of it until the last minute. I was furious with my father when he accepted her hand from the Bottaros in my place, but I can see now why he did it. He knew I'd be enraptured with her, no matter how much I fight my feelings.

The one thing that confuses me, though, is that he's preached all along about the importance of not having a weakness. Violet can easily become mine, if she isn't already. She sits next to the man at the very top and she's young, naïve, and inexperienced. She doesn't have the strength just yet to be where she is. If that isn't a weakness, I don't know what is.

My fingers move to pop a few buttons of my shirt free, loosening the neck area. The air hits my chest and my hands switch to rolling my sleeves up, exposing my tensed forearms. "Now, get to your knees," I demand.

"How about I sit on the bed?"

"I expect you to kneel before me. Now do it."

She huffs, pausing to argue. I know she wants it, that my bossiness gets her wet. I've seen the evidence from the very first night that I stole her virginity. That's right, I stole it. I wasn't about to allow another man to have what was rightfully mine.

Does that make me a bad man for doing so? Who fucking cares. Violet Vendetti belongs to me. I'm the Capo dei capi. Her life was bartered to me in place of her safety, and I keep my deals. When it comes to the life of the mafia, the organized crime of the underground, civilian rules don't apply, especially when it comes to me. People have this disillusioned fantasy that we're all good men underneath these expensive suits. We're not. We're criminals, feeding off breaking the rules. We lie, cheat, steal, maim, and kill, then you expect us to yellowbelly up and sprout romantic gestures? Not in this life, not here, and not if you expect to survive.

My tongue clicks, a tsk on the tip should she decide to argue. She shoots me a look full of heat mixed with irritation instead and does as she's told. That's my good girl. She'll learn with time. Eventually, she'll get it.

My gaze remains pinned on her, watching as she kneels before me. My sweet, prideful wife is at my feet and has promised to do whatever I wish of her after we visit her family. My lips twist up into a smirk, relishing every bit of this, loving that I'll be able to get what I want without being the villain in her eyes when we all know that's exactly what I am.

"Open my pants, Violet. Take my cock into your hand." My breathing increases as she unclasps my slacks, tugging the zipper down. She pauses for a moment, taking in a breath, staring at my solid black boxer briefs. My dick's hard as a bat, every nerve in my body eager for her touch on me. With a swallow, her hands move to work my pants over my hips.

"The boxer briefs, too, mia fiore. You can't jerk and suck my cock if it's covered." She could, but it wouldn't feel nearly as good. Besides, I enjoy watching her obey each order far too much to stop myself.

Her dark irises gaze at my form with curiosity, and it reminds me that she's most likely not had the chance to previously look a man over as she is now. I'm up-close and personal for her perusal, bared and open for my wife. We've all fucked her, but she never once possessed this much control. Even when I had her on my lap, riding me, I was moving her how I wanted.

Violet bunches the waistband, tugging my length free of the restricting material. My cock juts out, anticipation thrumming through my thighs, eager for her to put me into her warm, wet mouth. "Wrap your hand around me, mia fiore, and stroke my cock."

She fists me, and I groan as she follows my instructions. Licking her lips, she moves her hand up and down, around and around, until my sack pulls tight. I don't want to come on her, but rather, in her mouth. "Suck me, bella." Beautiful is an understatement; she's absolutely enrapturing as she worships me. It takes mere minutes of her lapping and sucking my dick before my body tenses and my cum floods her mouth.

Placing my finger under her chin, she releases my spent cock and my brow rises. "Now swallow it down." She does so immediately, her tongue darting out to swipe the remainder from her lips.

Once again, I'm reciting a silent prayer for strength, needing every bit of help I can get to not roll over and offer her everything her heart desires. This is exactly why I'm head of the familia: I can keep my mind straight, no matter how difficult it may be. Violet certainly is a woman who's far too tempting. She makes it much too enticing to just fall for her.

Reaching down, I grasp her bicep, helping her climb to her feet. She's been quiet since our chat in the SUV, no doubt thinking everything over. It's a little unnerving, however. I like it when she's chattier. Her quietness has me wanting to tiptoe, and that's not my style when it comes to anything. "Grazie, mia moglie."

Her face softens and she offers me a subdued nod.

"A blowjob has you quiet? I was beginning to believe nothing would take the fire out of you."

She swallows, meeting my curious stare, "I'm just surprised." She shrugs a shoulder, tilting her neck side to side, stretching the muscles.

"Si?" Of what, I want to ask and pepper her with questions, but I hold myself back.

Violet nods and I tuck a long, inky lock behind her ear. "I enjoyed it a lot more than I was expecting," she admits, and I cough as she catches me off guard.

My eyes widen. She thought she'd hate giving oral? Now it's my turn to be a bit surprised. "Did you think you wouldn't? Enjoy it, that is?"

"I didn't know what to expect. I've wanted to kiss your body, touch it and lick it..."

"And?"

"I wasn't sure if you'd enjoy it. I don't know what I'm doing, and you're used to more experienced women."

I can tell she's not fond of admitting her feelings, and my black heart skips a beat at her apprehension.

"Those women were nothing— a means to an end. You, however, Violet, are not only my present but my future— my wife. You mean something to me, and I would very much enjoy you doing all of those things to me."

Her lips turn up, cheeks a bit warm and flushed, and it's so damn endearing. I must've said something she liked to get that type of response from her so easily. Her smiles make my chest grow tight and emotions swim through me whenever it comes to her. It should be too soon for me to care so greatly about her. On one hand, we're barely getting to know each other, yet on the other she's already my wife. My thoughts when it comes to her are enough to give myself whiplash. I guess it's to be expected growing up with Romano as a father.

"Can I kiss you?"

A scoff escapes me. "Of course. Why would you think differently? We're married." Of course, I don't need to remind her, but in this instance, I feel it suitable.

"I meant after I...you know."

A lightbulb comes on in my mind and my mouth spreads into a wide, satisfied grin. "Oh. You mean can you kiss me after you suck my cock?" I love the sound of that, her sucking my cock.

She clears her throat and nods.

I find myself smiling even wider. I shouldn't find this much enjoyment right now but can't help it. I'm all man, and her blush has my chest tightening with ownership. "Of course. I'm not a prude, fiore."

She leans up on her tiptoes and my head lowers, bringing my mouth close enough for her. She keeps the kiss chaste on my lips, testing the waters a bit, but I don't mind. I like it that she's the one initiating our contact. It's usually the opposite: me taking what I want, touching her how I wish and telling her what to do. With her stepping up to kiss me, well, it's sweet.

"Tell me what I bargained for," she whispers, and I grunt. Violet's persistent, and it's a trait I admire, though not with this. She'll have to learn forbearance.

"I will, after we visit Chicago and see what we've walked into. I'm sure you'll want to discuss it in detail, and I don't have the patience for that at the moment. We need to focus on the task at hand."

She sighs but keeps her thoughts to herself. I'm not mentioning anything to her until we're back at the estate. She's had a vexing day, and after what's about to go down...there's no telling how she'll respond with more demands made of her.

A chime sounds overhead, alerting us that we need to be buckled into our seats. Violet looks to me and I nod. "Get dressed. We're most likely getting ready to land." I yank up my boxer-briefs and then my slacks, my gaze never leaving her as she fixes her shirt and pats her hair into place. Having my cock in her mouth and her swallowing my cum moments prior has the alpha in me feeling pretty damn satisfied. I doubt it'll be enough to dissuade my brothers for touching her though.

Once she appears to be back in order, I murmur, "All set?"

"Yes. I think so. I mean, I have to be, right? My family needs me."

"We can always go home, mia moglie. You owe no one a thing. This sense of loyalty you possess, the nature to help them as if you owe them for your life is endearing but completely unnecessary." If it were my decision to make, we wouldn't offer the Bottaros a second thought, but I'm leaving this one up to her. She needs to wise up eventually and realize her mother's not the nurturing type. I don't want our future bambinos around the old hag.

"Of course, it is. I owe them for my life."

The tsk slips from my lips as I disagree. "You came to me half-starved with threats on your life. That is no way for you to live. You owe nothing to someone who has you '*live*' in such a way." I should've had her parents taken to the basement and whipped for a small bit of retribution before allowing them to leave the estate.

"I could've eaten," she argues, stubborn to a fault.

I snort but refrain from rolling my eyes. "Si? Then why did you pass out? Why hadn't you eaten?"

"Because...I didn't want to hear my mother gripe. I didn't want to fight with her over it. She knew I was going to see my husband and wanted me thin when that happened. She obviously had a reason to not have me eat."

"Yes, because she is bitter; she is jealous of her own daughter. I should've killed her." She gasps, and I tug her out of the bedroom to our seats in the main cabin. Pulling the belt over her lap and then my own, I make sure we're both secure.

"I won't," I finally reason. After all, with her father dead, I'm ninety percent sure her mother is as well, and we're making this field trip strictly so I can get something else I want from her.

"I'm going to use the restroom before it gets any later. I need to splash some water on me or something. I just need a minute."

I nod and watch as she unbuckles and practically climbs over me to get out. That's fine; I could use a moment to reel my thoughts in as well. She's been with me for no time at all, it seems, and already has a healthy glow about her. When her family tricked her into coming to the estate, she was stunning, no doubt. She also looked a bit run-down and weary. Violet may not care to discuss her mother's treatment, but I only speak the truth about her. The old woman is jealous and spiteful of her daughter, and what better way than to chip away at her daughter's health and beauty. Hopefully, the pitiful bitch is dead when we arrive; it's the least she deserves.

Chapter 5

Can you remember who you were,

before the world told you who you should be?

- k.w.

Violet

"Violet? Santino's gaze meets mine as I move to step into the spacious on-flight restroom Matteo pointed out earlier. I had no idea it would be this vast. I was expecting the cramped little closet type you have on regular flights. This is far from it.

In fact, it could be a small bedroom. There's a custom, high-end ivory marble sink, toilet, full-sized shower, built-in vanity, and sitting bench. The vanity was no doubt designed with a woman in mind. Was it Romano, Matteo's father, who thought of it, or one of his brothers? I know Matteo would've never given it any of his precious time. The entire room is all plushy decorated as well, nothing at all like flying coach with my parents and cousins has always been. This is my life now...Can't say I'm disappointed in this small perk or any of the others Matteo's wealth has offered so far.

"Oh, excuse me, Santino. I was under the impression that the room was empty, since the door wasn't locked. I was going to splash some cool water on my face and attempt to pull myself together a bit more. This day has been stressful." I don't know why I find myself opening up to him so easily and rambling on with meaningless conversation. Maybe it's because he's the closest to my age, or his kind features, taking after Liliana. She had to be a strong woman to deal with Romano for so many years. Yet I guess, in the end, she couldn't handle him after all.

"It's fine, carina. Come here." He holds a hand out to me, open, drawing me in. In the moment, he seems much older, more experienced than I'd ever imagine him to be. My fingers land in his palm and he leads me closer. "Sit and relax. Let me ease some of this tension." Rather than allowing me to step to the side and sit next to him on the bench, he pulls me to him, having me straddle his lap. Things just got a whole lot warmer in here too.

A small smile appears at me from following his lead, a dimple to the right of his mouth showing itself. He's classically handsome, but what am I even saying? They're all so attractive, like someone out of an old movie. You don't discover men made up like them; they're cut from a different cloth.

I find myself mimicking his grin, taking him in closer. He's easily become one of my favorite people around the mansion. His easygoing attitude and friendly smile is inviting.

"How did my brother get so lucky with you? Hmm? Your beauty, carina, you take my breath away. We all notice it."

His name leaves me on a sigh. "Santino." I barely manage to get it out as his lips meet mine. He's so different than my husband, yet so much alike; all of the Vendettis are. It's consuming and overwhelming. Yet, I already find myself not being able to picture my life without them, and it's hardly been any time at all really.

Our mouths part enough for him to murmur, "I want you." It's all the invitation I need before moving to stand back up. Eagerly, I toe off the slip-on sparkly silver Toms I'd yanked on earlier, then shove my yoga pants off with a flourish. He does the same, impatiently opening his pants and shoving them along with his boxer briefs to his ankles. His large, strong hands rake over his thighs, knees spread, cock jutting forward as he stares at me from top to bottom.

"Turn around and sit on my lap, Violet. I want to rub your shoulders and feel all over your body while I sink inside your heat."

With a nod, I release a breath and peel the rest of my clothes off. Tossing them off somewhere, I spin around and sit as he requested. Santino guides me down over him slowly, positioning his cock at my entrance. The swollen head parts my folds, causing me to draw in a breath. He fucked me so hard the last time; will it be the same way again? Matteo's not here this time to watch us, to command my attention and demand my orgasm. Damn, that was a hot night. I love it when Matteo touches me with his brothers around. There's something so forbidden about it, like he knows it turns me on that he's watching them fuck me.

Santino wraps those strong arms around my waist and pulls me onto him, seating himself deep. "So, so good," he murmurs, his lips coming to kiss along my neck. He rubs them over the sensitive flesh, his hands moving to cup my breasts, tenderly squeezing and flicking the stiff peaks.

"Oh, Santino," I whisper. My body's bursting with desire, my breath's increasing, and he hasn't even begun to move me yet. "You feel big—really *big.*"

His chest rumbles, sounding pleased as he continues his pursuit, his hands rubbing up and down, over my chest, pausing to rest on my shoulders. He squeezes his strong fingers, massaging achy muscles I didn't realize I even had, and my head tilts in submission. His hips rock slowly, up and down, up and down, his knees under my own, spreading me wide open. I'm so full of him. These Vendettis have huge cocks. There's no way I can only think that either. They really must be oversized to be able to still fill me up so much after having sex multiple times.

The door handle moves, the door clicking as it's opened, and I draw in a surprised gasp. I forgot to lock the freaking door! Santino pauses in his grazing mouth and thrusts to watch with me, waiting for whomever may enter. Part of me wishes it would be Matteo; I want him to discover me like this. Especially after seeing how furious he was catching me with Dante. It's wrong of me, but I enjoyed seeing him become so worked up. He was fuming and turned on, and it made me crave him even more.

Luciano pops his head in, cracking the door open. His brows rise as he finds me naked and sprawled before him, laid out on top of his brother. "Babe," he croons, his gaze growing molten.

"Come on in," Santino gestures with a wave of his hand as if we're at an all-you-can-eat buffet.

Luciano's smirk grows into a pleased smile as he further looks me over, this time at a more leisurely pace and much closer proximity. "You two are in here all closed up, fucking like rabbits, while the rest of us are on this boring flight."

I can't help but stare at the pronounced bulge in his pants. He's turned on seeing us like this. He was the one who was biting and demanding my attention, and it seems as if he's ready for it again. That first night some of them fucked me was unbelievably hot. If only I'd have been as relaxed then as I am now, I would've been in even more pleasure than I already was. To have all seven of them come at me now, I'd have my arms spread wide in welcome, eager for the touching and the orgasms I know would be offered with their resilient, attractive bodies. Judging by their muscles, devilish looks, and massive dicks, you'd swear I married into a family of gods. I've never wanted to worship more than I do now, either.

"You want my cock, too, Violet? You ready for both of us?" he asks, catching my gaze, and my cheeks flush. Of course, I want him too. I want them all, after what they've opened my eyes up to. Any woman in her right mind couldn't get enough of these dominant men.

I nod, biting the inside of my lip as Santino begins to slowly move his length inside me again. The feeling has my body shivering with the need to come. Matteo wouldn't allow it earlier when I was sucking his dick, and now it's like I'm this bomb wound up and waiting to go off. I have not one but multiple Vendetti men within reaching distance, and two of us are already naked.

"Come here, Luciano," I call with a breathy purr, finally finding my ability to speak on what I desire. Santino's hands begin their exploration all over, kneading my breasts and plucking at my nipples. My thighs shiver, my juices pouring from my opening onto Santino's length and groin.

With Luciano's pleased groan, I yank him a step closer, enough so that I can undo his slacks and yank them down over his cut hips. He's not wearing underwear, which explains why I could see him so aroused and ready to join in. I could make out the head of his cock, he was so hard in his pants. "Can I suck it?" I ask, already putting my newfound experience to use, wanting to taste him.

"Fucking shit, beautiful Violetta. Yes, you never have to ask to put my dick in your pretty little mouth."

Pushing Luciano's pants down a bit farther, I use one hand to lead him between my lips, opening my mouth wider to take in his size. The other hand moves to cup his balls. I give them a soft squeeze before rubbing my fingertips over them as Matteo had liked. It works as he grunts in pleasure.

Santino spreads my butt to seat himself a touch deeper, and we both moan in response. Luciano threads his fingers in my hair, moving my head how he desires. Relaxing my jaw as much as possible, I take everything he offers while losing myself in the feeling of Santino between my thighs as well. This is what I mean by overwhelming. These Vendettis take over every bit of you, mind and body, until all you see everywhere is them and no other.

Moments pass us, me wrapped up in the heat of the two of them. I lose track of time. I was only supposed to be coming back for a minute to splash water on my face but couldn't hold back from their inviting touch. In the next blink, Luciano's nearly purring in satisfaction as a long string of Italian comes pouring out. In the same instant, his warm release hits my mouth. He empties himself, reveling in the pleasure as I slurp down every delicious drop with a flourish that takes me by surprise. Who knew sucking their fat cocks would be so fulfilling? I love the small bit of control surrendered from them.

Fully sated, his passion-glazed, sparkling irises find mine. He pushes me backward a touch and Santino responds immediately, pulling me in flush to solid his chest. His shirt has to be completely ruined by now. One shoe is missing also as he's kicked free of one pant leg at some point to give him more range to piston his hips. With him holding me back against him, my body's wide open for Luciano's hungry gaze. He may have just come, but he definitely enjoys the sight before him. I watch, panting and cheeks hot, as he kneels before us. Santino's feet hook around my ankles, spreading my legs open as far as possible, and then Luciano's leaning in. Head between my thighs, a gasp spills free as he laps hungrily at my clit. His mouth moves with an enrapturing pace, the pleasure rushing from my core through every nerve ending.

I can't hold back any longer. I was a ticking time bomb, waiting to go off. Having their body heat and scents surrounding me is dizzying enough that after being so close to Matteo earlier...my mind is only focused on the Vendetti males. Luciano flicks his tongue as Santino sinks his teeth into my shoulder and I scream out with release. My pussy spasms, clamping Santino's cock hungrily. I need to come like I need my next breath, and with Luciano's face between my thighs licking my pussy and Santino's heavy cock driving into me again and again, I finally allow myself to fully succumb and let go.

My orgasm swipes through me like a tidal wave, a tsunami hell bent on leaving a lasting impression. The greedy clenching of my cunt forces Santino to finish right along with me and spill himself deep inside my sex. He roars into my shoulder through his own blissful completion. With heavy breaths, I feel remarkably satisfied. I just pleased two men and in return had one hell of a potent orgasm.

"Damn, babe," Luciano pants, "you're getting fucking good at this already." He wipes the back of his hand over his brow.

Santino chuckles, hugging me tight to his frame one last time. "Agreed. Any more practice, and she'll have us all trailing her like trained soldiers. The Capo wouldn't be fond of the lack of control, that's for certain."

Luciano climbs to his feet, holding a hand out to help me stand. I'm grateful for his thoughtfulness as I'm a bit wobbly. "Do you think that it's wrong for me to enjoy it so much, being intimate like this with you all?"

Luciano grows serious, his hand lightly trailing over my jaw. "Hell no. We all want you to love it. Pretty sure I can speak for each of my brothers, too, when I say every one of us want your attention and affection."

"He's right," Santino confirms as the three of us move to get dressed again and fix ourselves.

"You may want my attention, but how do you guys feel about me enjoying my time with every one of you? Does it bother you that I've had sex with the seven of you?"

Santino moves to stand right behind me, fixing my hair a bit better with his fingers. The locks are messy. Between laying my head against him, and then Luciano wrapping his hands in it, my hair didn't stand a chance. Not that I minded in the slightest. I love when they yank on it a bit; the tiny bite of pain mixed with their caresses certainly heightens the experience. "Of course not," he responds. "We know what is expected of us. I can understand how it could be a bit confusing to you. The main thing that I believe you keep discarding is the small detail that we were all raised this way."

Luciano's head tips in agreement, his Italian brogue all caresses and sexy rumbles to my ears. "Si, we knew that one day Matty would be the Capo dei capi and marry. Romano told us of our brother's future wife and how we would be permitted to share and continue to pleasure her if she wished us to. We also were made very aware that you may choose to only be with all of us once for tradition's sake. It was mentioned that you may prefer to be with a specific brother multiple times and not another. We've known this since we were boys— twelve or thirteen I'd say. So, to answer your question, no, it doesn't bother any of us. We're glad you are enjoying yourself. This is your life. We want you happy and content, always, especially Matteo, even if it may not seem that way."

"Thank you," I breathe, a bit relieved. I don't want them to be jealous of each other or think poorly of me because I enjoy all of them. Moving to the sink, I wash my hands and face in an attempt to remove some of the puffiness from my earlier crying. Grabbing a fresh towel, I pat my brow and mouth dry. It doesn't cure the sad, strained expression, but paired with my recent orgasm, it does make me feel a bit refreshed.

"You are the Vendetti Queen, Violetta," Santino continues, sounding confident and sure. "You are most important to us, aside from our brother." His confident admission has my gaze training on his.

Tears crest, as their words fill me with warmth and comfort. Matteo may seem a bit cold at times, but I'm beginning to understand it. He has to be that way; the man is in charge of so much, so many people, and an abundance of money. His responsibilities would make a weaker man easily give up and cave. It's okay, though, because while my husband may be new at this relationship stuff, as am I, his younger brothers are here to help make up for everything he's not showing me. I think with time he will eventually warm up, and even if he doesn't, at least I understand why he is the way he is. He's the mob king in an empire full of crooks, cons, and murderers— I'd be pretty fucking icy myself.

***

Matteo

Dante leans over the small walkway between our seats and into my space to speak to Violet. "Are you feeling better, bella?"

Before she can reply, I growl low, close to his ear in warning. The fucker is in my space, speaking to my wife after I'm already irritated about the two of them fucking earlier. "I should have you whipped," I threaten with a hiss, and he turns to me with his own glower.

"You may be my Capo, and I respect that, but you are not Romano, Matteo."

I meet his stare, fury enlightening my irises with painful, unspoken promises and take him down a notch. "Exactly, Dante; I'm worse than Romano ever was. Remember that, when you take it upon yourself to fuck mia moglie, *soldier.*"

He huffs but gets the message loud and clear, sitting back in his seat. The aisle isn't far enough between us at the moment, in my opinion. Right now we could use a canyon between us so I could have breathing room and cool down. I don't want to even look at him, not until I can fill Violet with my seed, replacing my younger brothers'.

Violet leans in. "Matteo, he didn't do anything wrong. I wanted him just as badly as he wanted me," she admits softly, and my eyes fly to hers. My hands begin to shake at her revelation. Of course, she wanted him. I knew that deep inside, but to hear her say it...

My shaking fingers raise, two covering her mouth. "Shh," I murmur. "If I hear you say any more, I may kill him and the others— my own flesh and blood. I know you were with Luciano and Santino in the bathroom and I almost cannot handle myself at the moment. Being keenly aware that your silky thighs are sticky with their seed rather than my own, it, well..." I exhale unsteadily, rage about to tip over and consume me. "If I get too carried away, I may kill you as well, wife."

I don't know what has me admitting it to her outright. I'm stupido, a bastardo for doing so. The last thing I need is to frighten her and push her away, but like every other powerful Capo before me, I feed off the fear from others at times. Maybe it's good if she's just a touch fearful. Hopefully, it'll make her think next time before she tells me she wanted my brothers' cock inside her.

Violet swallows, with wide, alarmed eyes appearing even more striking. Soundlessly, she nods and drops the raw subject. "What's the plan when we land?" She's clever, altering the subject, and it works, lifting my mood a bit. If we're lucky, the killer will still be there, foolish enough to wait around for mia moglie. Mia familia can clean house and knock out two birds with one stone: the Bottaros and whichever familia believes it's resilient enough to take their place by force. I'll spit on them. Good riddance to the watered-down blood, in my opinion.

Of course, I don't say that aloud. "There will be a few vehicles waiting for us when we touch down. We'll get to your parents' house and my men will infiltrate the premises quietly. They'll take out any threats and let us know when we may go in and inspect the property."

"But what about my mother?"

She'll be dead, by either the killer or one of my brothers. That I can almost guarantee.

"What about her?" I ask, tracing her impeccable jawline with my finger.

"I have to go inside to save her."

I manage to hold back the sneer wanting to break free. "Who told you this?'

"I told you earlier that I received a phone call with directions on what I needed to do to help her."

Grunting, I remember perfectly well what she'd said earlier. "Fine. My men will enter first. Once I have some sort of an update, my brothers and I will escort you inside."

"I'm supposed to go in by myself."

"Of course you are," I drone. Every shmuck with half a brain would've told her that. "No, mia moglie. Think like a Vendetti, like the queen of The Empire."

"I have to keep myself safe," she reasons, and I nod approvingly.

"You're the most significant person in this familia; you're our future, bella. Always think of that first. It's why my mother made sure my father had our portraits on the way to his office. He always had to keep us, his familia, in mind before making any rash decisions. You're going to have our sons someday; you may be pregnant as we speak. It's too early to know that just yet, but you must remember your obligations."

Violet sighs, looking away. She stares off, lost in thought, wearing an invisible weight upon her shoulders. I'll leave her alone for now. She has a lot on her mind, no doubt. With time it'll all become less taxing— second nature, even.

 If not, then it'll be her own personal hell.

Chapter 6

She made broken look beautiful and strong

look invincible. She walked with the universe

on her shoulders and made it look like a

pair of wings.

- I love you mom quotes

I gave in and allowed Violet to go inside without me. She assured me that she'd be careful, and I trust my men along with Santino and Luciano to keep her safe. She pleaded her case, reminding me of that backbone of hers I'd spoken so fondly of before, and like a putz, I rolled over for her. As long as whoever was in the house waiting doesn't put a bullet in her as soon as she enters then we'll be good. I'm still questioning myself on what the hell I was thinking, but Violet has a way of bargaining with me. Is it because she's a woman? *No.* Perhaps it's because she's my wife, I'm attempting to be considerate of her needs. Also there's the small bit about me getting what I want when this whole charade is over with.

Glancing at my cell, it's still black with no update, so I decide to send Salvatore and Cristiano a quick text, checking in. Unlike Santino and Luciano, the two of them back home respond immediately. I put Cristiano on babysitting duty; I know Salvatore will pass out at some point. I'm only worried about what he'll get himself into until that happens. At this rate, my seventeen-year-old virgin brother may be more accountable than half my brothers.

Maybe he could handle the Chicago seat in another year or so. I'll have to keep him in mind after all.

Valentino interrupts with a grumble, "Out of all of us, she gets you to give in. For the record, none of us agree with this."

"You're in love with her, aren't you?" I question, getting straight to the point. He's been damn near obsessed with her since she stepped foot in the door. So have Dante, Santino, and Luciano. The only two not completely under her spell seems to be Salvatore and Cristiano.

"She's your wife; it's my duty per our familia to look after her."

"You didn't answer me."

"You're being irrational and overbearing. You're the Capo, you're in charge, and we all know this." He waves me off and my cheeks heat, holding my temper back.

"Damn it, Tino. Tell me if you love her."

He huffs, flicking his gaze back to the house. Violet and the guys went in about five minutes ago. We better be getting an update soon. I was expecting one at the two-minute mark. I wanted to go in with her, but the men had me stay back as a precaution. I don't like it, but I do understand that all of us can't head in at once, especially her and me. What I want from Violet is enough for me to concede this once and allow her to go on in without me. It won't be that way in the future, however. After this deal, she'll heed my orders just as everyone else does. She belongs at home, safe and secure.

"In love with Violet? Not in the sense you're thinking. At least not yet. I feel protective of her, most certainly. I want to see her smile, and I want to bed her any chance she'll allow it."

"What happens when she tells you no to the fucking?"

"Then I'll respect that and protect her with my life. I know the rules; the tradition was drilled into all of our heads, as well as yours. You may have the wife, but I'm well aware of what's expected of me when it comes to her."

Nodding, I leave the conversation alone for the time being. We need to get tonight over with before anything more can be discussed anyhow. Rubbing my hands along my slacks, I pull the glock free from my custom-made shoulder holster. I threw it on before leaving the house, and in this instant I'm glad for it. I doubt there'll be any threat left after the guys are done clearing the house, but you can never be too careful, and I prefer to be able to protect myself at all times. Checking the fine piece over, I release a pent-up breath. "I'm tired of waiting. You know I prefer to do my own work."

"Me too," he concedes, pulling his own gun free. He checks the chamber then gestures outside. Nodding, I move soundlessly, exiting the vehicle with him hot on my heels. We're both highly trained killers; you'd never see or hear us coming unless we wanted you to. It's refreshing getting out of the house to do some groundwork. I haven't had my hands dirty since I took the trip to Milan. I'd been leisurely hunting the Empires' enemies, taking them out leading up to becoming Capo.

I'm stunned my phone hasn't vibrated yet to let me know if we have the all clear. I can't imagine what could be going on inside for it to be taking this long. I wasn't anticipating anyone to be here at this point. I thought maybe one guy left behind to try and take a shot at Violet as well, but that's about it. Clearly, that's not the case as various lights are on, the residence appearing as if the Bottaros are still alive and well. My guess is that they've already begun to decay and the call was bogus to draw Violet here.

The house and surrounding property isn't nearly as big as the Vendetti estate, but it's still pleasant. I'd guess the sprawling home has eight or nine bedrooms, along with a five-car garage. The landscape is done up in a variety of shrubs, flowers, lighting, and many umbrella-cut trees. It all surrounds a circular driveway along with the black iron fence spanning the entire residence. I'd never been here before this trip. I've visited Chicago many times, but not the Bottaro home. We were enemies, as far as I knew, so we kept our distance and they kept theirs. Or so I thought. Apparently, my father was in contact with them to arrange the marriage and for who knows what else.

Valentino comes to stand beside me, silent, brooding. His irises sparkle, taking it in. It's been awhile since he's had fun as well, the last time being when he slit the man's throat to discover which order he'd get to fuck Violet in. I should've known it would be him. I'd had my guesses and he was at the top. Another reason why he's my right hand: he's quick and takes after me in the mafia sense. We kill similarly, and we both have good business sense. I'm proud of Tino, even if I don't share that with him.

"New plan: we go in there and find out what the hell is going on. Any sign of a threat on her, put a bullet in whoever crosses us. I'm done being patient, sitting in the car like the wife. Mia moglie should have her sexy little ass in there with men surrounding her, not be in the midst of any danger. I should've told her no and left her in the car while I handled business."

He nods. "I like that plan much better. I have your back, Capo, whatever you need."

"Follow my lead," I quietly order and stride toward one of the side entries Violet pointed out to us before we arrived. Me and Valentino can sneak in and find out firsthand what the holdup is.

***

Violet

"Please just stay back. He won't hurt me," I plead with Santino and Luciano. They stand on either side of me, arms crossed, glaring. We watch the man before us, standing casually and regarding his handiwork.

My mother lay on the ground not far from his feet, blood everywhere. I can't believe he actually killed her, and that revelation also tells me that he murdered my father as well. It's surreal, witnessing my mother completely lifeless, her face twisted into her usual spiteful glower, even in death. She must've been scowling when he drove the blade over her throat and then through her heart. No surprise on her part, just irritation, I'm guessing. She was always so miserable; I never understood why she chose to be that way. My father loved her and even her children, despite how she chose to treat others.

"You don't know that," Santino argues.

Luciano interrupts, "He's killed your parents. This's too dangerous for you. You need to get behind us. It's our job to keep you safe, to protect you, babe."

"Agreed," the older man behind them says. I've seen him with Matteo many times. He's one of the mob soldiers who assists the guards around the Vendetti property.

"Just trust me," I beseech. "Matteo did, and I need you to as well— all of you guys."

Dante scoffs. "He would never agree to this. Our brother will kill us himself." He should know; his eye is already turning dark from the punch he'd received hours earlier.

Without another thought and ignoring their concern, I step from the shadowed area hiding the hallway. Holding my palms up, I carefully make my way closer to the madness and farther away from my protectors. Each step draws me nearer to the man who murdered my family. On bated breath, I offer a timid smile. Happiness is nothing remotely close to my emotions, but I must remain calm and collected as much as possible. I can stop this; I have to. I need to be able to make some sort of sense out of all of this, and that begins by attempting to talk to a man I don't know very well. He's been around my entire life, yet the only thing I've come to learn about him is that he's dangerous and unstable.

His devious gaze lands on me, and then momentarily flicks toward the darkness behind me. Hopefully, he can't see into the hallway and discover the small army of mafia soldiers waiting for any sign of duress. Matteo will be furious if he finds out that I've moved away from my safety net. His brothers are probably texting him at this very moment, telling him I'm disobeying their orders to stay put.

Exhaling, I try to reason, "You promised me you'd wait. You said to find a way to get here, and here I am. I kept my word, yet my mother is already dead." My voice cracks on the last word, no matter my effort on remaining unperturbed.

He smirks, his handsome face so very cruel. I always believed he was evil inside, but never to this degree. "Violet, I knew you wouldn't disappoint me as they have. You've always been perfect in my eyes."

A tear trails down my cheek at the mention of my parents' disappointment. They'd let me down too, damn it, but they didn't deserve this fate. I want to scream and throw stuff. I want to call him a killer, a murderer, and tell him he's the lowest piece of filth to kill someone's mother and father in cold blood. I refrain, knowing I have to remain composed. It's the only way I'll stay alive.

While we've never been close— never been allowed to be— I know this man well enough to be aware just how much of a loose cannon he can be. I've heard the whispers from my cousins and the staff. I'm not stupid enough to believe they were lies, when I can see the unhinged look of desperation and madness swirling in his eyes. I'm next on his menu; I know it without having to hear him say it.

The questions come peppering out in lieu of my anger, my hurt and frustration toward him. "What have you done, Alessandro? Why?" I just want to scream and pound on him— fuck! He's careless, rash, crazed. He never deserved to be named after my papa.

He shrugs. "I suppose since the old man is dead, I can let you in on a little business. I heard our father discussing his retirement. He wasn't going to put me in charge. He was speaking such nonsense."

More tears cascade down as I remain quiet, waiting and listening to his pathetic excuses for eradicating his own parents— my parents. He killed them in cold blood, yet here he is, unfazed over his actions in the slightest.

Fucking sociopath.

"I heard him say that when he retired he wouldn't appoint me in his place. That he'd be handing over our respected family chair at the five families' table to the filthy Vendettis. The plan was for one of the brothers to take our father's spot when the time came, to infiltrate the Vendetti Empire into Chicago. Apparently, it was a piece of the agreement he struck when he gave you up to them. Those Vendetti rats want it all, Violet, don't you see?" he rants on.

"When does their reach of power end? When do the smaller families stand up and say enough? It's time someone stronger took over."

"And you're that man?" I question my older sibling. As much as I want to mock him, it would be an instant death sentence. He's even more deranged than I'd previously believed. He killed our parents for disappointing him. Pretty goddamn entitled, and I'm the one coming up on my twentieth birthday, not him. He's older, more experienced... crazier as well.

"Of course, sister. I wanted you to get back here so I could save you from that family. It'll be me and you, the Bottaros of the future. We'll take over everything and become the most powerful mob name in the states."

A real Bonnie and Clyde fairytale, let me tell you. He's delusional to think I'd ever have anything to do with him after this. Let alone what my husband would do if Alessandro attempted to take me from him. The nonsense of us becoming more powerful is ludicrous; it's one of the reasons why my father offered our seat. He was well aware of our name compared to the Vendettis', and Matteo could take our place and have a real influence. He did it for my future, not because he was being careless toward my delusional brother. This was something he could offer my husband, an incentive with income involved to help my future. My poor papa... I wish I'd known he'd struck this deal for me.

"I told you to stop this nonsense when we first arrived at the Vendetti estate, Alessandro. You're my brother; I can't be with you how you want me to. It's wrong!"

He scoffs, waving my statement away. "It's father's fault for keeping us apart like he did. It only made me desire you more. How could I possibly look at you like a sister, when we weren't raised as siblings are? You've been a treat just dangling before me, forbidden, and then to have father hand you off to that family...I swore to you that day I'd get you back home. I meant it."

A sob escapes. He's sick. He's not right in the head; he never has been. That's the real reason we weren't raised as siblings, why we were kept a part so much. It was because my father didn't trust my safety alone with my older brother. He was smart to think that way, as his cautious nature and shadowing over me kept me safe in my own home from Alessandro Jr.

"This can't happen, Alessandro. I'm married to Matteo already. It's too late. You know this." He was there, not at the actual wedding as my father wanted to keep him far away from me during such a charged moment for our family.

He reaches for my hand and I offer it willingly. I'm no threat to him or the spot he wants to claim. He can have it, as far as I'm concerned. I only wish to bury our parents and mourn their deaths in peace. I want to attempt to move on from this horrifying event and live the life I've been given from my husband. Obviously, there was a bigger plan set in motion by the Almighty, in allowing my arranged marriage to go through without a hiccup. Perhaps this is all part of a bigger plan for my life. I need to embrace my husband as his brothers suggested. *I need my Matteo.* My parents are gone. My brother may be physically well, but he is dead to me inside. The Vendettis are all I really have; they are my family now.

With a forceful tug of his wrist, I stumble the few small steps to him. Swallowing nervously, I seriously hope it doesn't alert the mob troops. I'm attempting to diffuse this situation, not make it worse. One move to alert Matteo's brothers and awaiting men, to make them any more anxious, and my brother will be made aware of their presence.

One of his hands flies to the nape of my neck; he moves quicker than I would've imagined for an insane man. He tugs my face close to his, breath hitting my throat as he croons near my ear, "I'll erase him from you inch by inch. After I'm finished with having my way, you'll never think of him again. It'll be as if he never existed to you in the first place. You will always be mine, *sister.*"

Swallowing down my gasp, my eyes clench tightly, fingers curling into fists as I choke the tears back. He wants me to worship him as if he's the new mafia leader already, as if he's the one at the top. Alessandro's nothing of the sort; he's no one compared to my Matteo. He's exactly the type of man my husband deals with and wouldn't bat an eye to put down.

What would the Vendetti Queen do? The thought hits me and my resolve comes around full circle as a plan hitches. *Take action; be the Queen and protect yourself.*

He has to release me or this won't work. "Please," I whimper, coming off as fragile as possible to him. I'm always the weak one, the sweet, innocent young woman who must be kept safe and yet craved by monsters of men. Maybe it's my fault after all; perhaps I draw them to me unknowingly.

"Yes, beg me, sister. Start on your knees. We'll remove that husband of yours from your mouth, firstly. Then we'll take it inch by inch from there."

Expelling a breath, I nod, curling my shoulders forward. Meekly giving in, I need to gain a bit of distance to breathe. "You have to release me, Alessandro, please," I remind him, and he chuckles.

With a harsh flex of his fingers, he squeezes my neck tightly like I'm a damn mutt in trouble. "Yes, of course. Remember what will happen to you next if you misbehave." He tilts his head toward my dead mother and I gag to myself. My poor mother. She was foolish enough to love my brother so much. He was her faultless child, and in the end it was her death in disguise. His hand skates from my neck to my shoulder, pushing me to stumble down to his feet.

I go easily, bending to him, and rather than stop, I fall farther, bowing to him completely, feeding his ego even more. It's ridiculous, and to anyone from afar, I'd look absurd. I don't care; it's exactly what Alessandro craves.

He hums in delight. "Yes, you are impeccable, indeed. Bow, sister, bow."

My hands slide under my body as my forehead rests on the carpet, completely exposed to the wolf in sheep's clothing. *Or is that me?*

"Rise, my beautiful future," he exclaims, hands spread to his sides, palms up as if he's some powerful being.

"Yes, Alessandro," I answer clearly and shoot upward. My hand swings around and up with the movement. My right hand grips the small blade I'd gotten off Matteo before leaving him in the car. I'd placed it under the elastic of my yoga pants waistband right at my hip. I have no pockets and didn't think I'd have easy enough access to my bra if I'd kept it there.

My brother's not expecting the weapon or the change of pace. He's far too entranced in my surrender, in my show— so much so, that he's in no position to stop the stab. Using every bit of strength and momentum I can possibly gain, I plunge the knife right into my brother's excited groin. It'll never fuck another woman for as long as he lives. He should never underestimate his opponent; Matteo recently taught me that.

He shrieks so loudly, it echoes through the vast living area. Blood floods through the front of his pants, and I scramble backward, still on my knees. He takes a shaky step toward me, his face contorted in a rage that has me terrified. I can't help but worry that I didn't sink the blade deep enough to stop him from assaulting me.

"Bitch!" he shouts murderously. His hand reaches for me; my own shocked scream reverberates noisily as a loud shot rings out. My brother's head flies backward with the bullet's impact, his body soon following and falling uselessly to the floor.

With a sob ready to break free, my gaze darts toward the hallway. My husband, of all men, strides ominously out of the dark. He appears more powerful in that very moment than I'd witnessed before. He's absolutely furious, I can see it, yet his movements are composed and controlled. "No wife of mine has to worry. I will always come for her," he promises, his stare finding mine.

My shoulders drop in relief. "Matteo," I gasp, and he nods, putting the weapon back in his shoulder holster.

"I didn't get an update, so I came to handle it myself. I won't leave mia moglie to handle men's responsibilities." He advances the few steps left to me. I'm down at his feet, gazing up at him from the floor. I can't help but be thankful it was him who saved my life. I put myself in a dangerous position, believing I could talk my brother down, yet failed. Matteo pulled through for me, not only by sending a search party out to find me on the side of a road, but then to bring me to Chicago, and now by saving my life.

His palm shoots out, open, welcoming for me. I place my own in his and he helps me to my feet. His thumb carefully swipes the wetness from under my eyes. "You are so brave, mia moglie."

"More like stupid," I counter and glance off to the side, unable to hide my embarrassment.

Matteo's finger halts, his free hand comes to my cheek, tilting my face so I meet his gaze again. "There is nothing remotely stupid about you, mia bella Violetta. You are brave to sit at an enemy's feet, to be vulnerable and strike like a snake in waiting. It's what made me fearful of you on our wedding day."

I snort. I can't help it, though. "You? Afraid of me? Matteo, you're this huge, powerful mob boss."

His lips tilt, his gaze soft and affectionate as he stares his fill. "Yes fearful, my love. You could've been a snake waiting to strike me. You're in my very bed; it can be a bit intimidating."

"I just can't believe you'd ever consider someone like me a threat... You're-you."

"And you're everything I needed and didn't know it." He shrugs.

I bite my lip at his caring admission, not wanting to look away and break the moment. This mess has to be cleaned up, whether I want to do it or not. People I once called family bleed on the floor around me.

I swallow and move to step away but he holds me steady. Coming closer, he leans in and places his nose to mine, grazing lightly as he whispers, "You're so fucking brave. I'm proud of you, my little queen."

Annnnd I'm crying for an entirely new reason now. His approval is everything. I had no clue I needed it, but having it has my chest tightening with emotion. "Matteo," I whimper and his lips move to mine. They take over, drowning all words with feelings. His mouth wordlessly showing me he cares deeply, mine responds by letting him know that my heart is giving in, that he's filling it bit by bit. He's so cold toward everyone and everything, yet he burns me up inside and makes me want to be better for him.

"You just killed him," I stammer when we pull a part. "It all happened so fast. How did you know where to shoot, that it would hit him?"

"My existence has been living the mafia way, growing stronger with each day that I got closer to being Capo. Your brother may have been disturbed enough to frighten you and even your father, but not me. There was a reason your father sought mia familia out for your security. Alessandro Bottaro is nothing compared to me, carina, mark my words. As for where to hit, well, I've been killing men for as long as I can remember. Alessandro's only saving grace was having you so close to him. I'd have preferred to slowly cut each of his organs free, witness the shock in his gaze as it registered, and felt the warm, gooey slickness of his watered-down blood coat my hands. Even then, it wouldn't touch on the type of death he ultimately deserved."

My stomach churns at his description. My mother's lifeless frame lay only feet away from my brother's now dead body. They both stare off into oblivion, haunting my memories. The realness of it all is so unbelievably overwhelming. I wanted Matteo's help, needed it, but was I expecting him to go this far in the end? I suppose I probably was. He's a monster; I've known that from the very beginning. He didn't become the Capo dei capi for the most notorious crime family by helping the homeless. No, he earned his spot from being ruthless, from being Romano's shadow.

Rushing from the room, I throw the closest toilet lid open and expel the contents of my stomach. There wasn't much there from the crazy day, and it's definitely empty now. A large hand comes to my back, rubbing rhythmic circles.

"Sweet bella, are you okay?" It's Santino. Of course, it is. He's become the friend I never knew I needed.

Flushing the toilet, I lean over the sink, washing my hands and face; tears coat my cheeks. The emotions finally begin to overtake everything: my mind, my body...I feel like I could just crumble into a ball and hide out in the dark until it all passes me by. I won't, though. My family is gone and I need to take my husband's advice more than ever. I need to be strong. A queen doesn't hide away; she takes her place and straightens her spine.

Patting my face dry, I lay the towel on the sink and then stand to my full height. Turning to Santino, I draw in a deep breath and get my emotions back under control. "I need to call my father's lawyer and get this placed cleaned up for the funerals.

Santino's gaze widens in surprise, and he nods. "Whatever you need, Violet; we have your back."

Coming into this family a month ago, I'd never have thought I'd be on the receiving end of those words, and they've never sounded so good. I'm going to need Matteo and his brothers to help me stand up straight through this. After all, a queen has her army, and with the Vendettis, it appears I have mine.

<u>Chapter 7</u>

She has been through hell.

So believe me when I say, fear her

when she looks into a fire and smiles.

- e. corona

A month passes us by with Matteo busily finding his place as the new Capo. The brothers— and everyone, for that matter— offer me space to mourn my family properly. I've lost so much and in a short span of time. Amongst the other changes, it was beyond overwhelming. I like to think of myself as a somewhat strong woman, but when your parents are murdered and your life completely changes, it's enough to throw anyone off. I'd grown up being called a princess and fully aware of my father's mafia ties, but it never impacted my life as it has now. I had no depth of the true weight those titles bear. It was a rude awakening and has opened my eyes a great deal. I have greater respect for my husband and his brothers, along with the loyalty they continuously show me and each other.

I've needed time to myself to grieve. While I may not have surpassed every stage in the process of grieving a painful death just yet, I'm getting there. The anger stage hit me almost immediately, right after denial. I hated anyone and everything— Alessandro most of all, even my papa and mother at some times. At this point, I'm not fully to acceptance, although I try to push myself in that direction. Frankly, I'm not sure if I'll get that far anytime soon, but I'm doing my best each day to come to terms with the things I cannot change. In my life, that list tends to be long and messy.

I think the fact that my father will never have the chance to be a grandfather is what's hammering me the hardest at the moment. He may not have been the best papa while I was growing up, but he tried. I have a feeling that without my future children being directly in the line of his work, that someday they would've loved him beyond measure.

I'm also confused with my feelings. I'm unbelievably angry with my brother, yet I still find myself mourning his death. Is it wrong of me to be sad that he's dead as well? I should hate him for being the source of my pain, but in death, I need to offer forgiveness, even if I don't completely want to.

"We have things to discuss," Matteo states calmly as we enter a spacious, nearly empty room used for office space. It has the necessary table, chairs, and beverage station, along with a few random paintings, but nothing else. I've explored the mansion with Santino and Valentino numerous times, yet this is another room I've never discovered before. It makes me wonder how many others there are hiding around here. This place reminds me of a palace more and more with each passing day. On the plus side, I can now find the kitchen, dining room, breakfast nook, Matteo's office, and my bedroom all on my own.

No one needs this many rooms. It's not practical, even if you do have seven sons to fill it. Santino says it was initially built with the intention of the entire family living here. Not surprising; Italians like to be near each other. Their heritage is quite family oriented when it comes down to it; so much so, that most of us can't stand half of our cousins, as if they're our siblings. On the contrary, if one were ever crossed, there'd be a bus load coming for whoever wronged them.

"Remove your clothes and climb onto the conference table, mia fiore," Matteo continues on, distracting me from my thoughts, and I catch my breath. The man has a way of always keeping me off-kilter when I'm around him, no matter what the situation or place is.

"Excuse me?" Another thing I've learned in the past month is to not be afraid to speak up when it comes to Matteo. At first, I had no clue what to make of him, his unspoken rules, and ways of his life. He comes off controlling and pigheaded, but as long as you approach him respectfully, he will return the curtesy.

"It's time you tell my brothers good-bye, in a sense."

The breath whooshes free as my mind races. Holy shit, this is what he wanted? He tricked me! "The terms?" I immediately guess aloud, and my husband nods, eyes twinkling with victory. He knew what he'd wanted all along and had planned for it. I treated him like a shark, and in the end, he was cunning, taking full advantage of the situation. He's waited, biding his time while I grieved, and now he's ready to collect.

I can't believe this was what he'd planned when I pledged to do anything for his help. My husband is indeed the Capo in the sense of striking deals. He told me I came to him, treating him not as my husband but as the Mafia boss he is, and in return he's shown me what that entails. I can't deny the blatant truth in that statement. This is exactly what a loan shark would do— what Ruthless Vendetti would do. "Holy shit," I mutter, and he gestures to the table with a flick of his wrist.

"You're good." I point at his muscular chest that I know is hiding under his finely threaded, long-sleeved button-down. The man does not do casual wear ever. He's either representing a GQ model or else he's naked; there's no in between. "I never would've assumed this is what you'd ask me for when we struck a deal."

"I'm not asking." The asshole shrugs. "You owe me a debt and now I'm collecting," Matteo confidently states. He takes a seat at the head of the overly large table that could no doubt fit at least thirty rich, corrupt men around it comfortably. "Salvatore and Cristiano will not be joining us. I made them aware of our agreement and they do not wish to participate. It seems that they aren't quite as attached as the rest of my brothers. Shocking, as I'd expected those two to be smitten the most with your intoxicating innocence."

"Did I..." I begin to ask if I screwed up with the two of them somehow. I never suspected I had upset them or offended them previously, but you can never be too sure with powerful men.

Matteo shakes his head, setting me at ease in that aspect at least. "No, you were perfect— are perfect. They have other things that consume their attention. Cristiano for example, is too young to grow attached just yet. My brother Salvatore prefers his liquor over anything else, which I'm sure you've come to notice being around us all so frequently. No worries, though, they will still protect you. The tradition is in full effect in that sense. They've pledged their lives to your safety."

My teeth release the bottom lip I hadn't realized I was chewing on. "I understand. I'm grateful for their sacrifice."

His mouth turns up, his eyes illuminating a touch as he nods in approval. With the age difference between Matteo and me, I can't help but to seek his approval. I believe it's the age gap anyhow. He's older, mature, experienced, and I'm none of those things in comparison. To witness appreciation and pride when he looks at me, it sends my heart soaring.

The Vendetti brothers promising to protect me doesn't come lightly by any means. Being married to the Capo dei capi almost guarantees that at least one man will give up his life to protect me at some point.

My responsibility, my contribution in the beginning of our relationship was nothing in comparison if they end up sacrificing their lives for me. Or even if they merely keep me safe for the rest of my life and remain alive, the duty will be immensely taxing on them and their own families, should they have them. Sure, I never would've thought that way at the time, but I recognize it now. I see firsthand just how much my father kept me away from everything. I never understood the danger, but the Vendettis are an entirely different level.

"Bella?" Dante stares quizzically at me perched on the end of the table as his bulky, brooding frame enters the room. His stacked muscles flex with each step he takes, and I swallow deeply, knowing what's coming. I wish I could've forewarned him. Dante's been coming to me more and more lately, making sure I'm okay and that I have remembered to eat enough in all of my grief.

"Take a seat, Dante," Matteo orders, and his brother does so immediately, preferring to fold his bulk into the chair to my left. I'm sure it only angers his older brother more, to show that he believes to be my protector, while Matteo will always be in the space to my right as my husband. It's opposite for us, as I'm always on Matteo's left side. It's the spot closest to his heart and his 'right hand man' sits to his right. I think it's a bit ridiculous to have a specific place to sit when it comes to your significant other, but according to him, a queen has her thrown. When he puts it that way, I can't help but seek out his left side each time. Perhaps the title is growing on me after all.

Santino enters next. Sending me a flirty wink and friendly smile he teases, "Ah, carina, should've known this was the reason to be summoned. You were causing trouble again?" My eyes roll and an unladylike snort erupts causing the man in question to chuckle. He usually greets me like this if I'm not the one to ask him to go somewhere. He pulls out a chair beside Dante; he and Luciano are constantly near him. Santino's so handsome, always the easygoing brother out of them all who can effortlessly bring a smile to my face.

Luciano glides in next, a man with all the time in the world it would seem. He glances to the oldest, casually nodding. "Capo," he says before his inquisitive irises land on me. "Babe?" I can understand his interest; I'm not typically around when Matteo calls them in for business. It's not that my husband has kept it from me; I've just been distracted with the death of my family.

"Hi, Luciano." I smile a bit timidly, not fond that I'm about to tell them all at the same time about my deal with the Capo. Luciano sits beside Santino as I'd expect; they're thick as thieves. Santino leans in and the two of them whisper back and forth quietly to one another.

Valentino, last but definitely not least, enters. He strolls to claim the spot to my husband's right. I guess I know whose side he'll ultimately take in this matter. Not that it'd be up for negotiation at this point anyhow, but still. I'm not too sure how the other three men will react, and I probably would've said that about Tino as well, before I saw him sit in that place.

"Capo," he acknowledges, and Matteo exhales, spreading his hands out on the table before him.

I stick out even more like a sore thumb, perched on the table like a display. Not to mention I'm the only female in the room. *It's not uncomfortable or awkward at all.* I cross my arms.

"Mia bella moglie, Violetta, has struck a deal with me in return for my help last month. She'd begged for me to take her home immediately the night she'd stolen the car and so recklessly drove off without any protection. In her pleads for my generous assistance, she offered me anything I wanted in return. *Anything.*"

There are multiple sharp intakes of breath coming from around the table, and it makes me feel even more careless for striking a deal with Matteo the way I had. I wasn't thinking, at all, and he's using that fact to his advantage. A smart man to a fault, no doubt. I won't make the same quick judgments in the future, even if I don't mind his stipulations this time. It's a lesson learned on my part.

"She has no idea of the significance, nor of the consequences of such a deal as that, especially when being made to a Capo dei capi," he needlessly supplies, for my benefit only.

The others already know what I offered up. I was foolish to not see it then, but I was under pressure and needed a solution immediately. Thankfully, he's gone fairly easy on me this time, considering all the many things he could demand in payment.

"What were you thinking, bella?" Dante quietly growls to my side, and I wince. He's the rational hothead taking after Matteo, and not only that, he commands respect as his older brother does as well. I don't enjoy disappointing any of them. I know he's only worried for my own sake, but it sucks to put him in that position.

"Given that she is so innocent in her promises, and then witnessing her bravery to take down Alessandro, I've decided to go much easier on her than I probably should." Matteo's offering is a weight lifted off their shoulders, but not mine. I know what he wants, what I must give. Not that I don't want to be with him, because every fiber in me does want to. But there are other ways to go about this. He could've let me come to him on my own, but he's a typical Italian male in that sense— impatient and determined to have his way.

Santino mutters, "Sweet Mother Mary and Joseph." He's making the sign of the cross in thanks. I don't have to witness it to know it's happening; I can hear the gratefulness laced in his tone. I hope this doesn't end up hurting him; I couldn't bear it. He's become such a good friend to me. He's almost taken the place as my best friend and in this circumstance, in this house; I would claim him just that. His loyalty and obedience is firstly offered to his Capo, but I'm confident that he enjoys spending time with me as much as I do him.

"There's also the matter of her being mia moglie; that works so favorably for her," Matteo continues, as if the fact of me being his wife means I get it easier should immediately be obvious. It's not; however, he may go easy on me in this moment, but he hasn't been so lenient in the past. "However, a debt made must be a debt collected, when it comes to the Vendetti name. In saying that, I've decided to keep her." He shrugs as if it solves everything.

Valentino's brow scrunches, his handsome face confused as he peers at his brother. "Keep her, Matteo? But she is yours already. Were you going to get rid of her? I was under the impression she was to have the heir." His smoldering gaze hits mine momentarily before landing back on his brother. Valentino has a way of drawing me in, like a spider with a web. I blame it on his cologne that smells so damn good it could be its own brand of crack. When we're alone, all I want to do is sniff him and possibly lick the hard set of abs he possess.

"I'm not going to knock her off, Tino." Matteo's hand waves the idea off as ludicrous. "When I say I'm keeping her, I mean that I am no longer sharing her, brothers."

"But the tradition," Dante and Luciano both say in unison, and my husband's chest rumbles with a possessive growl that screams alpha male. He's the king ding-a-ling around here and everyone is fully aware of that fact.

The room's immediately cast into a silence so stark, it's uncomfortable for everyone but Matteo. If I'd have to guess, I'd say he thrives in tense situations. His voice comes out eerily low, laced with anger as he carefully chooses his words. It appears as if Ruthless is right on the verge of breaking free and punishing the lot of us, and Christ, there must be something wrong with me because it turns me on seeing him this way.

"I don't give a *fuck*," his tone drops to a near whisper on the curse, "about the *tradition*. I was raised on that tradition, on being placed in this position amongst our familia. Now, my *younger* brothers will *obey*, as they have been raised to do so. Violet Vendetti is my wife, my queen, and soon the mother of my children. She made a bargain, and I will collect what is owed to me. *If* she wishes to have one last time with each of you, she shall do so here, now. Afterwards, anyone caught touching *my* wife in an unbrotherly manner will have his hand cut from his body, and frankly, I may leave you to bleed out at the utter lack of respect."

My throat is suddenly feeling a bit tighter than a moment ago, parched with his threats. I don't think any of us know how to respond to him laying down the law so clearly and without any room for argument.

Valentino says nothing but gets to his feet and storms out. That's his usual reaction when it comes to something that has to do with me though. He seems to be a bit explosive like his eldest brother, yet can't rein it in as well. Romano can be the same way, from what I've heard. I'll miss his heated touch and the spicy scent of his cologne that I could easily become lost in, but there wasn't more than that fiery sexual tension between us. If you take away that budding attraction, he's just another Vendetti brother and not the one I desire the most.

"This is bullshit, Matty," Dante attempts to reason, keeping his voice calmer than we all know he's really feeling. "Think about it."

"Is it though?" my husband asks with his head tilting, almost mocking.

I've already seen him straight up punch Dante, and that was nerve-wracking enough. I like to believe Dante has enough respect for Matteo to not speak out against his wishes. I can only imagine the carnage if the two of them went at it. I can't believe I've done this to them, created an unnecessary rift. They were all in sync with each other when I first showed up. Now, they're in sync with me.

After a moment, Matteo questions, "What if she was your wife? Would it be bullshit then?"

Chapter 8

Chin up princess or the crown slips.

- YourTango

Violet

Dante swallows, his stare jumping between me and Matteo. He seems a little lost at the moment, and every bit of me wants to pull his massive body to mine and comfort him. "Dante, please," I nearly plead with a sorrowful whisper and reach my hand out to him. He jumps back from my touch as if I'd burn him. His irises churn with a storm brewing as he gives me one last, long look. It's like he's trying to see into my heart, hoping to discover he has a reason to fight for me. Unfortunately, he doesn't, as it's always been Matteo for me, from the very moment I saw him in the club out in Milan. I wanted him then and I want him now, even more than before.

"No," Dante rumbles at me, full of emotion, and turns, locking his stare on the Capo. "I need some space, some time to regroup and breathe."

The oldest nods, almost as if he was expecting the request. "Of course. Take a week, and if you need longer, call me."

"Grazie," Dante mutters and stands, spinning on his heel to heed his exit. He's out the door without a backward glance in my direction. I won't lie, it stings. He's so fierce; he makes me feel safe whenever he's near, and now he's left so quickly. I don't want him to fight it. I never wanted to bruise their relationship, but damn, he didn't even utter a good-bye after everything.

Matteo regards me with sympathy. I was expecting more victory shining in its place, but the cockiness is nowhere to be seen at the moment. "You'll have to excuse him, mia fiore. It appears as if my brother was falling in love with you. It's better this way. He'll see that soon enough."

How can he know this? It's as if Matteo is much older than his actual age at times. Tears crest at my husband's admission. *Dante was falling in love? With me?* How is he aware of Dante's feelings and yet I wasn't? I had no idea. "Are you certain?" I question after pausing for a moment in my thoughts.

He nods. "It's always a possibility when it comes to the tradition. That's why it usually only lasts the first night. With you it was different. We had to pace ourselves, be easy on you."

A drop falls over my cheek, but I quickly swipe it away. I hate it that there's a possibility that I've hurt Dante in some way. I swallow, hoping to choke back a bit of the emotions. *I'm supposed to be strong, damn it, remember?* My spine straightens a bit, even if I don't feel as resilient as I need to be at the moment. No wonder they built this house so damn big; there was a chance for one of the queens falling in love with multiple men, and of course, they'd all live in the same place. How had I never considered this before? Matteo's not having it, however, so there's a chance that this living arrangement could be uncomfortable, just as I was believing that I was in the right place with each of these men.

"Don't feel guilty, Violet. Dante knew better. It's been drilled into every single one of us to not fall for the queen, whoever she may be. Even I'm supposed to hold myself back a bit, and yet I've been unable to do so. We knew the rules, what was required of us, but we weren't anticipating you," he admits, and I swipe away another tear.

Now they're all showing feelings for me, and it's tearing me up a bit inside. I don't want any of them to be upset, most of all Matteo. I made a promise when I first came here that I would give him my loyalty and not cause trouble. While I have pledged myself to him and have lost myself to bending to his will, craving his approval and affection, I've also stirred up trouble amongst the Vendetti brothers.

"I didn't mean to hurt him, for him to fall in love with me. I promise, Matteo. I would never want any of your brothers to go through pain."

"I know that; we all do," he consoles as Santino and Luciano both nod, solemn expressions marring their gorgeous features. "Do you, ah," he clears his throat, "love my brother in return?"

"Dante?" I ask, not expecting him to enquire or even care for that matter, and he confirms. "I do, but not in the way he seems to love me. I love them all in a way, especially after our trip to Chicago. They're continually trying to keep me happy or make sure I'm comfortable, safe, or fed...whatever need, I may have. They do their best to sate it. How could I not love someone— even just a little bit— who cares for me like that? My own parents never offered me such a luxury or that amount of affection before."

"Agreed," he mutters, his emotions shuttering before me.

I don't know what I could've said to make him go blank suddenly. He's been closed off from the instant I met him, but he seems almost hurt as well. My big, strong, mean Capo is wounded. Is it because I admitted to loving the Vendetti brothers in my own way, to loving the others as well as him? Surely, he cannot be that jealous already. The man has a possessive streak like no other, the spoiled Italian.

Santino and Luciano glance at each other one last time before standing. They step up next to me and each offer a warm hug. If I hadn't slept with them, I'd look at them in the respect of brothers, I suppose... but not the type that are psycho and kill your parents. Although I have no doubt that if I'd have desired them to kill any family members, they'd be the ones I could ask without any judgment being returned. Not only favors to that extent, I know I can count on them. They have good hearts, and in such a dark lifestyle, it's a hard attribute to find, especially in two people at the same time.

My palms come to rest on their clean-shaven cheeks, my stare switching between the two handsome young men so close to my own age. "I'm sorry," I admit, my forehead wrinkling in guilt. This should've been done privately so I could've explained to them that I love them in my own way but that I also made a deal that I have to keep. In the end, I know this would've all come to a screeching halt regardless, and it's better sooner than later for it to happen. However, I wasn't expecting it to go down in this very moment.

They offer me sweet, kind smiles, both leaning in to place a chaste kiss to my forehead. Santino pulls me into his chest, murmuring, "I pledge my life for yours, carina. I'll always be here when you need me. It's time you give my brother the chance he deserves."

I nod, too choked up in the moment to reply without my voice cracking, giving away my emotions. They're both young and amazing; they'll find wives of their own quickly. Our time together will be a memory, one that no one ever speaks of again. So help me, those wives better treat them like princes, too, or else this queen will show them just how strong my Capo has made me become.

Luciano embraces me next, his palm coming to rest on the side of my throat. The touch is so intimate, not brotherly in the slightest, but I have to stop thinking of him in any other sense. "Santino's right, babe," he agrees. "Matteo sacrifices so much for his familia. If this is what he asks of you, then give it your whole heart. Don't worry about any of us; we all knew this would happen sooner than later. I think we were all fooling ourselves by keeping it going longer than was necessary. You belong to Matteo. Let him love you in his own way."

"I don't want you guys to hate me." My lip wobbles. I wouldn't be able to look at myself in the mirror if I knew they hated me for this. It was never my choice in the beginning, yet in the end, it was all me. I wanted them. I enticed them and enjoyed every moment of our time spent together.

Luciano steps back, his other hand moving to embrace the opposite side of my neck, and he stares at me dearly. "Never babe, never. We all have your back, as we do our Capo's as well. We want what's best for you."

"I'm going to lose all of you guys. You've become my friends, my family." After my parents' recent murder and the showdown with my brother, well, family seems to be dropping like flies around me. I can't stand the thought of losing any more.

"We are your familia," he murmurs. "But now, we are your brothers. Nothing will change between us," he consoles, and my husband speaks up.

"Except no fucking...or touching...or kissing."

"Right." Luciano nods. "Everything else will be the same, that I promise you."

Releasing a breath, I pull him in for one last hug. "Thank you. I'm so grateful for all of you. Crazy, I never thought I'd catch myself saying that, but it's the truth."

"Si." He grins and bows his head to Matteo before leaving us in silence.

Matteo

She sits there, seemingly a bit broken. Her lip trembles and her innocence is everything that's alluring to a man like me. I want to break her, but she's pretty fucked-up already, she just hides it well. In the past month alone she's been handed over and married to a man she didn't know— a hard man at that. She's been fucked from here to Sunday by six men. Cristiano never succumbed to the tradition, but she'll never discover that. Mia fiore believes she's fucked seven men in the last month. To top it all off, her parents were murdered in cold blood, she had to stab her brother and then watch me kill him not two feet in front of her. Now she's learning that deals made with the Capo are always paid up. I'm Ruthless, always. Wife or not, she has to pay her debt. The devil always collects on his deeds— always.

"They will treat you the same. You have trust them. Dante may be a bit standoffish at first, but give him some time," I suggest, uncertain how to offer her the consolation she requires or deserves from me. The truth is that I have absolutely no idea whether Dante will fully come around. He'll protect her, that I have no doubt about whatsoever, but for them to be friends like she is with the others? I can't answer that.

Perhaps I'll put Dante in the free seat back in Chicago that the Bottaros used to fill. It would do him good, but do I really want him that far away? He already loves Violet. I know he could end up being one of her fiercest protectors if needed. I'll have to think on it. Salvatore could never go as he'd be too much of a liability; I'd be far too worried he'd end up dead or starting a war. Cristiano, on the other hand, would be perfect if he weren't so young. As far as my other brothers, Santino and Luciano, I need them here. They're the level heads I require around me to help balance out myself with Cristiano and Salvatore. Valentino is my right hand, and he's proved it even more so with Violet around. He's the one I can count on no matter what. I thought it was the others, but he's proven to be my strongest asset.

"When I made that deal with you to help me, I never would've imagined this is what you'd want in return," she repeats, no doubt in shock just a touch. She doesn't have small life changes; hers seem to be big and immediate.

"Si?"

Violet nods, her eyes curious as they take me in sitting below her. I don't like looking upward at anyone, my wife included, so I stand.

"Tell me, mia fiore, are you sorry now that you know? That my terms were revealed and set in motion? That you will only warm one man's bed?"

She shakes her head, her teeth sinking into that plump dick-sucking bottom lip of hers that I adore so much. "How could I regret anything when my husband wants me for himself? I'm almost wishing I'd struck some sort of deal with you sooner. Had I known this was going to be what you wanted, I would have figured something out."

My mouth lifts into a smirk and I move a step closer, coming to stand next to her thigh. Gazing down into her sparkling irises, I admit, "Not sure I'd have requested it sooner, so it's a good thing you were stubborn enough to hold off. In the future, however—"

She interrupts, "I won't hesitate to tell you when I need something, and if the situation calls for it, I'll take action. I'm stronger now,

Matteo, I promise. I think what you were trying to tell me finally sank in."

My smirk grows, pride shining from me at how much she's evolved in such a short amount of time. "Good girl," I comment, my thumb lightly lifting to graze along her jaw. She's so utterly stunning it makes my chest ache. The need to possess someone has never hit me as strongly before as it does with her. She's mine and only mine. Just as I'm hers, she's had me from the beginning, and I had no clue.

My hands move, shoving her dress over her tanned, shapely thighs. With each inch of exposed silky smooth skin, my cock grows harder. I want her even more, knowing she's only mine. Strange, I'd imagine it'd be the opposite, but that's not the case. This woman, my wife, will only have one man inside her for the rest of her life— me. I was her first and I'll be her last. The knowledge is so unbelievably empowering, it makes her all the more enticing in my mind.

"Wait," she murmurs, her dainty hands falling atop mine to slow their perusal. I'm so much bigger than her in every way. She's feminine, and I adore treating her so, being her protector.

"What is it, carina? Let me have you."

"I'm not finished discussing this."

"I am."

"Please," she whispers, and I exhale, taming my dick for the moment. She wants to talk; we can debate this now so it's not brought up later. I figured she'd need to go into it deeper, and that's exactly why I didn't bring it up when we were flying to Chicago. That and because I didn't want her to have a chance to think over it too much or to admit she'd fallen for my brothers.

"Very well, what more is there to speak of? We had a deal: you owed me in return, and I've told you what I want. You're mine alone, and I'd like to see you grow with mia bambinos immediately."

"Yes, fine, Matteo. You want my compliance, and I promised it already. However, I have my own terms, if you want me to be on board fully, especially when it comes to getting pregnant immediately."

"Si?" I grumble, flicking my curious gaze over her.

Nodding, she continues. "I will have your children and I will do everything I can to be the best mother possible to them. However, you must promise me something in return. What happened to me will not happen again; it cannot."

"What are you talking about, mia moglie?"

"I'm speaking of the betrothal. How I was checked by Romano. You can't do that in the future."

She acts as if it's all my doing, but it was my ancestors who put it all into play. My father would never allow me to alter our traditions. He'd figure out a way to quietly take me out and make Salvatore, my impressionable brother, the Capo. It'd be the perfect plan for Romano's type of influence. "Fiore, it's nothing I can control; it's tradition. We do this for a reason. It's necessary— "

She interrupts, "No. Hear me out, please. I understand that it's a tradition and an extremely important one to your family— our family. I even understand the betrothal process, but there's one thing I won't stand for."

My brow raises. I want to argue but refrain and stay silent to hear her out.

"The way I was checked over by Romano...we will not put another young woman through that humiliation. You will not allow our son to do that to another woman when he meets her. I won't stand for it, Matteo."

Inhaling a deep breath, I pause a moment, thinking over her terms, and choose my words carefully. I want this agreement too badly to not give her an inch. "She must sleep with him the night of the wedding, along with any other sons we may have. I'm unable to change that detail."

Her dainty hands shoot up, placating. "I understand that part, the significance. After this time with you and your brothers, trust me, I get it. I agree with you. As much as that may make me seem like a monster being a woman, I understand the importance of it. With time you've grown more and more possessive. I won't have our sons fighting over a woman, attempting to have her fall in love with one of them first."

"Good, at least that's something we can both completely agree on."

Chapter 9

Some old wounds never truly heal,

and bleed again at the slightest word.

- George R.R. Martin

Violet

"So I will do this, what you ask, but in return, you need to promise me that you'll never touch our sons' betrothed. Never allow him that power to embarrass and humiliate the woman, especially before he even knows her true character."

I watch as his jaw flexes a bit from his teeth clenching. Clearly, I've struck a nerve, but I promised from that moment Romano had his fingers in me that I'd make sure Matteo felt retribution from it. Here, the man finally cares enough for me to demand I be his alone. I know it's the perfect opportunity for me to make my displeasure from the beginning known. Of course, things have changed. Hell, they altered for me the moment I saw his expertly sculpted face and felt his alluring presence...and then discovered he was the man in Milan I'd craved so desperately. He's the one I'd fantasized about multiple nights, unknowing that he was due to be my husband. I wonder if I would have felt the same, had I known who he was and what significance he'd play in my life.

Many may see the arranged marriage as wrong. I was one of them as well, prior to being married to Matteo. However, it's our way of life. Not just for me, but for many women who grow up attached to the life. It's ironic how the men in the underground break the laws, making their own way, yet they're traditional when it comes to marriage and families. Being around the Vendettis has opened my eyes so much to the importance of true family and loyalty. Their bond is stronger than any other I've seen before; it's no wonder they're so influential. Each person in this family would give their life for the other, and that makes them a deadly combination. They'll do anything to strive, to persevere and come out ahead.

Matteo finally answers, running his finger along my jaw. It's something I'd expect Santino or maybe even Valentino to do, but it's so unlike Matteo. He keeps offering me increased bits of care and compassion, of warmth, and dare I say it, love. I think my husband's falling in love with me, and that's a very potent feeling to have. They've offered me glimpses of power, of control, and I find myself craving it bit by bit as time goes on. Maybe I'm not so different from these men after all. Perhaps I fit in so well with them all and right away because I have more in common with them than I'd originally believed.

"You have my word, mia Violetta. I will teach our sons to be more respectful, to show more trust than I did with you when it comes to their future wives. Heed me on this, though, *moglie*, it will only be towards their betrothed as she will hold the Vendetti name. Any and all others, no matter that they are females, it does not matter. They will be viewed as a potential threat to our sons and to all of us. While I respect you keeping their dignity intact, we're a very sought after familia. We're on many hit lists, and our familia's safety is the upmost importance. So while, yes, I'll concede on not touching our sons' future brides, all others will be a threat until proven otherwise."

I release a breath. It's a lot for him to give in and agree to my demands. Realistically, he's the Capo dei capi. He could tell me to shut the hell up and not listen to a thing I say. If he wanted, he could lock me up in a basement if he so wished. Luckily, he hasn't gone to those extremes. Matteo's that powerful thought, and I can't allow myself to forget that now or in the future.

I'm also grateful because, while I don't mind him sharing me with his brothers, there's a piece of me that's unbelievably jealous when it comes to my husband. I haven't let him see that side, but it's there. I don't feel that sense of possessiveness when it comes to the others, but Matteo *Ruthless* Vendetti is all mine. I've put up with way too much of his shit to settle for anything less. I promised from the very beginning that I'd make sure he'd fall in love with me and eat his words and actions. What I didn't count on was falling for his impatient, selfish, pigheaded ways in the process.

"Then fucking breed me," I relent, muttering breathily, and he moves suddenly. He has me so freaking turned on with all this negotiating and the amount of respect he's offering me. It has me wanting to rip his clothes off and demand he lick my pussy while he's giving me what I ask for.

The chair slams off to the side onto the ground behind him. It's ridiculously noisy, but none of it matters. I only have eyes for him in this moment. There could be gunshots and screaming and I wouldn't break the stare I have on him. He's so imposing and bad and unbelievably flawless, I can't get enough. I thought with him being an asshole Capo that it would turn me off, but it's done the opposite. His spoiled, demanding tantrums have me wanting to push his buttons more and more. A tiny piece of me wants to see the Ruthless side of him. I have a feeling I'd end up liking it, and that's just a touch scary, if I'm being real. I'm a bit twisted inside, and being with a man like Matteo makes me appear like a damn saint; it makes me seem not so bad after all.

He reaches into his fancy blazer, coming back with a long, thin, tan leather strap. Gripping it in one hand, his palms fall to my thighs, the leather nearly burning my flesh with anticipation.

"What's that?" I ask. I know what it is, but I need him to tell me what he plans on doing with it.

He yanks me closer to the edge of the table, busily scooting my dress up the rest of the way over my waist and then pulling it over my head. I'm left in a baby-blue lace bra that really covers nothing, it seems. The material's so thin, it rubs against my nipples, mimicking foreplay over any sort of support.

"Matteo?" I probe breathlessly, and he grins. The man actually grins as he grips my wrists together.

"It's leather, watch."

And I obey, my gaze trained on his hands holding my wrists together in front of me. He carefully wraps the leather over them, making sure only the flattest part is against my skin so it doesn't pinch as badly. With both of them secured together, my palms flat, he quietly orders, "Wind your fingers together to make one big fist." I do as he says and watch him bend down to pick the chair up. One large palm comes to rest in the middle of my chest as he easily pushes me to lay flat against the hard, boardroom-style table. My hands stay in place, tied together over my stomach. Tilting my head to the side, I watch as Matteo sits in the chair and scoots it all the way to the table, my legs spread eagle on either side of him. He can easily see everything, including my pink folds that seem to be getting wetter by the moment.

"I thought we were going to fuck?"

"We will," he replies, not looking away from the juncture between my thighs, "but first, I want to feast."

He yanks me to him until my ass is near the edge, my pussy right up close and personal with his upturned mouth. There's a sharp intake of breath, and he nearly growls, "Bella, you smell so delicious. My mouth is watering just thinking of licking this pretty pussy." Then his mouth lands right where I need him, sucking my clit strongly. A loud, keening moan leaves my lips, not expecting such a brutal assault immediately. This is Matteo, though; I should've known he wouldn't eat my pussy halfway either. "Oh God!" I cry when he sucks again and pushes a finger deep.

His hand moves, fingering me hard and deep as I pant, attempting to keep up with the shocks of pleasure shooting through me. With a loud, sucking slurp, he releases my clit and I cry out. He flicked my clit back as if it were a rubber band, sending a tiny spark of pain to get me even wetter. I'm dripping; I can feel my juices running down my ass. He's getting me so fucking turned on right now, I want to yank him into me so I can ride his face. I want that clean-shaven jaw covered with my juices.

"Absolutely divine," he comments, licking the wetness from my thighs. "So, so good, mia fiore. Sweet and intoxicating." When he stands finally, his cheeks are heated with a light flush. My eyes train on his hands, his gaze molten as it looks me over as I watch him suck his fingers clean of me.

He's even proper in his compliments when he's eating pussy. Lord it's such a turn on. He's elegant and refined, completely on another level, yet so down and dirty and wild. "Your ass is wet, carina, soaked from your ravenous pussy, and it makes me want to fuck it."

I squirm as he touches me again, adding in two more fingers, spreading me open wide so I can take his huge cock. "Please, Matteo, I need you," I pant. My legs shake as I clench around his fingers.

"I know you do, mia bella Violetta. You don't realize, but you've had me from the first fucking minute." With that, he removes his fingers, replacing them with his long, hard length. One solid push, and he plunges in to the hilt. He must've freed his cock when his face was between my thighs because I never saw him do it, and I wasn't expecting his thickness so far inside me when he plowed deep.

"Oh, Matteo! I-I..." I lose the ability to say anything else as I'm overtaken by a quick orgasm. My pussy spasms, greedily wanting him to keep going, to not stop until our muscles have nearly given out with satisfied exhaustion.

He uses the leather restraint as a handle, gripping it as my wrists press firmly together. One of his hands hold the leather, the other grasps onto my waist, and he drives into my heat again and again. He's so dominant and bossy and beautiful.

"What shall I do to spoil you for your birthday?" Matteo questions out of the blue, eyes catching mine as sweat dots his brow. "How about orgasms?" he asks and tilts his hips, hitting that one button deep inside me that has me screaming and shaking through another orgasm, this one blinding, surpassing the last.

There was no slow build, no kind of warning, just zaps of bliss when I wasn't expecting it. My pussy squeezes him so tight, it almost hurts as his heavy cock thrusts in and out, hard and deep. His steady rhythm and my tight grip have him groaning. He's nearly breathless with me, an unusual feat for my experienced husband. Normally, he's chastising that I need to keep up with him, but not now. He was all in, his body straining while trying to hold his orgasm back, it drained him and made the rapture all the stronger for him when he finally gave in to the feeling and stopped resisting.

"Matteo," I breathe his name, and he nods, seating himself all the way, draining the last few drops of his warm, creamy cum. The pressure sends more mini shock waves through my core. My hips jump, my clit swollen and incredibly sensitive from his roughness, and I moan. He groans at the same time and then smiles. I beam back at him and he plants his mouth to mine.

It's official, I'm completely done for.

Using his elbows to keep the bulk of his weight from squishing me, he thrusts one last time and breaks our kiss, drawing back. His dick leaves me, along with the warmth his body was just cocooning me in, and it has me wishing we were in my bed, all wrapped up in the fluffy blankets. "We should go to my bed," I suggest immediately as he helps me sit up and pulls his pants back up. They along with his black boxer briefs had fallen down around his ankles.

"You need to move into my suite," he randomly mentions, and my brow scrunches.

"You want me in your space? You don't want privacy, or need it?"

His mouth tilts on one side, barely. "Of course, we are married. Privacy ended when we recited our vows."

Cheeky bastard. He's kinda cute too. Okay, he's really freaking cute. "I'm aware of that, but I thought men in your..." I clear my throat. "In your line of work, prefer to have an open bed." I hate the words; they taste rotten against my tongue. I swear if I find another woman with him I may lose my mind and strangle her. It would definitely break my heart, but I'm not going to fool myself and expect him to never take another woman. He's head of the Empire, he's the Capo...men in the life often have mistresses.

His hands cup my cheeks, a glower taking over. "I told you that you are mine. Only mine, Violet. You will have no other man in your bed, only me."

"I understand, Matteo. I gave you my word. I was talking about you." My gaze lowers, staring at the hardwood floor. It's the color of walnuts, hand-scraped, and looks insanely elegant for such a plain room meant for meetings.

He tilts my face so I have to meet his stare directly. He's no longer glaring at the idea of me keeping my own bed. He seems a bit thoughtful, if anything, like he finally understands the jealousy churning inside me when it comes to even thinking of another woman sleeping next to him in my place. "You are *mine*. I am *yours*," he says.

I bite my lip. I'm not fucking tearing up. I'm not.

His soft lips land on my forehead in a chaste kiss, and rather than dress me, he uses his blazer. He wraps the warm fabric around me, over my breasts, tying the arms of the jacket to hold it in place. It smells like him, strong and masculine. I wish I could bring it to my nose and just breathe it in, or maybe sleep with it under my pillow so when he's not in bed I can sniff it all I want.

There's one small issue, though: my hands are still tied together at my wrists. "Umm, Matteo?"

"Si?" His big palms span on the sides of my breasts, his thumbs under the perky mounds. He easily lifts me from the table until I'm standing steadily in nothing but my see-through blue lace bra, my

Jimmy Choos, and his jacket. I'm covered, yet fairly close to being naked.

"I'm still tied up." I hold my interlaced fingers up, not that a visual is necessary in this circumstance. He can clearly see my bound wrists in front of me.

"Oh, I know, bella. I've merely only begun to have my fill of you. And if you even think of arguing, I'll grab my ball gag from my office. It's right next door, and you know how much I enjoy seeing you wear it."

I flick my eyes in the direction of his office. I wonder what he'd think if I said it's what I wanted? He told me he likes when I'm bold, so I shrug. "So stop wasting time and grab it. Stop teasing me with these promises."

His eyes enlighten and a pleased growl rumbles his chest. He snatches the leather handle, using it to lead me out of the room. "Hurry up or I'll carry you, and if you kick, I'll drag you," he assures, and I grin.

"A new deal," I hum and suddenly sit in the middle of the hallway, pussy exposed for anyone passing through. My sudden move jerks his arm and he spins around.

Confusion and concern mare his face as he asks, "What happened? Did you fall?"

I almost laugh, but I want him to see I'm serious. "Nope, but the Capo just made a deal. I'm making sure he keeps it."

It only takes a moment for my meaning to dawn on him, and with a pleased growl he bends, lifting me up to hike me over his shoulder. He's careful with my bound arms, but I still manage a squeal as he swats my bared ass and rushes for his office. We're both far too eager to have our fill of each other, and it's the best deal yet.

Chapter 10

A sky full of stars and he was staring at her

- Atticus

Matteo

Severo pops his head into my office. "Capo?"

"Si, Severo...come in." I gesture to the empty chair in front of my desk and stretch my arms out wide. Crazy sex moves has muscles aching, reminding me of my gorgeous wife and her insatiable appetite for my cock any chance she can have it.

"You wanted an update about the bodies the polizia had found in the yard."

I nod. I've been waiting on these cops to figure out what they were doing ever since they announced they'd uncovered them. Sure my brothers are guilty of killing them, but we never would've left them to be so easily accessed. It was extremely messy work the way they were found. Someone was lazy, and it wasn't my men.

"They got a confession," he shares, further garnering my attention. It's about time some news came forward.

"Mm?" My brows hike with the shock. I was worried they'd be coming after at least one of us over the whole ordeal, since we hadn't heard anything sooner.

"I guess it got around that Ruthless Vendetti was looking for the bastardo. The lowly Mafioso wannabe that found the bodies stumbled on them by luck. The fella had stolen some shit, went to bury it, and boom, found one of the schmucks with their throat slit. He thought it'd be his chance to move up. The idiot then shot the guard."

"Makes sense why it was so damn messy." My nose scrunches, memories of my father's reprimands on not being neat and organized enough comes to mind. The bastardo wouldn't have ever pulled that had they grown up with Romano doing the whippings. He'd bloody you until you couldn't move without whimpering and tearing a wound open to freshly bleed. We learned our lessons quickly and efficiently.

"My thoughts as well. Once he caught wind of who wanted him, well, I guess he thought jail time would be a decent option. He confessed to killing them all. Your reputation precedes you, as he'd rather do life than attempt to live with you hunting him."

"I don't want him to have any time to change his mind."

"I'll arrange it."

"Good, make it a nice clean hit. The cops will never know it came from the Vendetti Empire, and the stupido bastardo gets what he deserves for killing that innocent yard attendant."

"Yes, Capo."

"Oh, and make sure Salvatore doesn't attempt to tag along this time. He needs to stay out of the way."

"I will, sir. Another thing..."

"Si?"

"Your brother." He pauses, seemingly a bit uncomfortable all of a sudden.

"Which one?"

"Dante."

With a sigh, I gesture for him to go on.

"He called for a cleanup the other night."

This is news to me. No one thought to bring it to my attention at the time, that's for certain. Vito steps into the doorway and I acknowledge him with a quick head tilt. He obeys, taking the seat next to his friend and fellow soldier.

Severo continues, "He was too rough with a..." –he coughs, clearing his throat— "a whore."

"He killed her?" I gape; stunned that Dante would be the one wrapped up in this mess and not Salvatore. Both men nod.

"Dante was on something. I don't remember seeing him like that since he was a teenager and Romano had went at him with a harsh punishment."

The memory hits me instantly. "Salvatore thought it would be a good idea to give him some new pills he'd been popping. Dante was trashed," I remember aloud, though it's unnecessary.

"He said the whore was talking about being his Vendetti queen, that she could be for all of you. Guess with that, he lost it. She slapped him and he strangled her." He shrugs and I shake my head. *Fuck.*

It's only been a few weeks since I told my brothers they could no longer be with Violet sexually. I thought they were handling it fairly well. We've been giving Dante the space he requested, and

Valentino was a little salty for a few days, but the rest didn't skip a beat with mia moglie. Was it the whore mentioning the queen spot or the part about having us all that triggered him?

"Do you know if he was on anything when he strangled her or if he took it afterwards?"

"I'm not certain, Capo. He sent us a text. I handled it alone, but Vito was around when I drove Dante home. He was in no shape to drive or stay at a hotel alone."

"Grazie, I can't believe he strangled a woman. Whore or not, she was a female, and it's not like my brother."

"He asked for it to be kept between us, but you may be able to find out more if you bring it up. I've been around you and your brothers for the majority of my life and yours; I don't believe he would've just killed her in cold blood."

"You think he was provoked and not in the wrong, and the drugs just happened to be in the mix?"

They both nod and Vito speaks up, "Mr. Vendetti, we were discussin' it." He gestures next to him and Severo tips his head, agreeing. "I was sayin' to Sev that maybe the whore gave Dante the smack or whatever it was he was on that night. Or he could've knocked her off and then found her stash, took it cause he was feeling guilty, ya know?"

"That could be a possibility. Dante's a hothead, always has been, but he's never that out of control or sloppy. I'll think on it. I'm not sure if I should bring it up or act as if I'm unaware."

Vito grumbles, "You being newly married and all, we don't want nothing coming about to put stress on Mrs. Vendetti. You need anything, we're the fellas to make it happen, sir."

"I appreciate that." Especially if she ends up pregnant. She does not need any added stress that my brothers, men, or the polizia could bring with foolish outbursts. Meeting Severo's stare, I order, "Talk to the men. Make sure they understand that now is not the time to be making mistakes. I will not be lenient, especially when it comes to upsetting mia moglie. Capisci?"

"Yes, Capo," they reply in unison, gazes trained to the ground in respect, and I excuse them.

I need to figure out what's going on with my brother. Maybe sending him away is the best option after all, regardless if I want him home or not. I don't know how else to help him move past this, other than to keep him busy. On the plus side, the incident with the bodies has been taken care of, so that's one less pressing matter to deal with.

"Cristiano?" I call. He's in a small room off my office. He's the youngest, so he's around me the most, learning the ropes of the familia. I wouldn't be too surprised if he just overheard the conversation that just took place either.

"Yes," he responds instantly, coming into my office.

"Any update of the Bottaro seat we were given?"

"I spoke to the head of the Morelli familia; they respect the word of Alessandro Bottaro and welcome a Vendetti to their table."

I roll my eyes and scoff. It's bullshit, but I'll play nice for the moment.

He grins. "I'm sure they're still silently cursing me. I have a feeling they'd flip their shit if even I went. I'm the youngest of the familia and they see me as a threat for their meager area."

"It's because the Morelli's are smart; they know we could come in and take over anytime we wanted. As long as our bank continues to get deposits from the Bottaro trust, we'll leave them alone. Once that stops, however, I won't make any promises. I was considering you as a candidate."

"But I'm seventeen!"

"I'm aware. Are you frightened?"

"No, of course not. Intimidated a bit, sure. They may not be as powerful as you are or as we are together, but alone, they are much more experienced than I am."

"That's exactly why I had you in mind; you're smarter than they are. You don't underestimate them, yet if they saw how old you were, they'd make the mistake of believing you a lesser opponent."

"I don't want to go, Matteo."

Not that I was planning on sending him immediately, but I'm curious why not. "Oh? Not ready to grow up just yet?"

"You know that's not true," he mutters, reminding me of my father when he doesn't get his way immediately.

"You're spoiled," I comment, never holding back from him.

He grunts. "I will go if you demand it. You know I accept my duty wholeheartedly. However, I was hoping to have a wife soon."

"You're young, Cristiano, take your time. I'm thirty-three and have barely wedded mia Violetta, what, almost two months ago."

"I wouldn't mind going to Chicago if I was married, if I wasn't stuck out there alone."

"You wouldn't be alone; you'd have plenty of men with you," I begin to argue but stop myself. He may be young, but after our discussion before about him saving himself, maybe he does know what he wants for himself. Who am I to tell him differently? In mafia standards, he's been viewed as a man for some time now. I never see him that way as I've helped raise him; he's still so inexperienced. "Fine, you want a wife, Cristiano? Well then, we will go to Italy and find you one."

"Italy?"

I nod, thinking that we can bring Violet and maybe, just maybe, we can have a little time to relax. Valentino can take care of things here for a few weeks if necessary. I'll have Salvatore with us so I can keep an eye on him. I'll also bring along Luciano for Violet's protection if she ends up going somewhere without me. It's a good plan. I'll find my little brother a wife and see him content.

"Why not someone from the States?" he asks, not thinking of our heritage and how things have been done for many years now.

"Because there are no familias here with daughters your age that fit your station."

"You sound like Romano."

I shrug the implication off. It's true; it's what our father would say. Though I am right. The only women who will understand our ways and are young enough for him are in another country. I know all of the prominent bloodlines here in the States, and no one matches his needs.

"You think there's someone in Italy that fits your requirements?"

"Mm." I smirk. "Actually, I know there is." One of the oldest familias, in fact, has a granddaughter that should be right around

Cristiano's age. It'll secure the Vendetti's more so then we are already in that country and they'll be happy to offer her up to our good, wealthy name. Although it may be an issue that we'd be taking her from her familia, we'll deal with it. "I'll make a call," I promise.

His normally serious expression lifts, a grin taking over. "I'll get to see my friend, too, if we're going to Italy."

"Who?" I don't remember him bringing anyone around.

"The florist's daughter."

That's right. He didn't have to bring her around, she'd come with her mother each week with the flower delivery. I'd only run into them a couple of times, but they must've been delivering them for our visits for years now.

"Concentrate on your future fidanzata, Cristiano. You want this badly enough, I'll make it happen." I'll do anything for my brothers, if it's with in my reach. I know he wishes to meet a young woman, fall hopelessly in love, and marry her in the church, but unfortunately, that's not our way of life. I can give him the woman and the church...the love part...well, he'll have to learn on his own to love his future wife.

Smartly, he nods and thanks me, rather than waste any time to argue for the florist's daughter. Hopefully, she won't be an issue when we get there. I'm sure my brother will take one look at his future and forget all about the past.

Chapter 11

The prince of darkness is a gentleman.

- Shakespeare

Violet

"We're going to Italy. Call it an early birthday trip," Matteo informs, and I immediately start nodding, agreeing. I've needed a change of scenery with the death of my parents. I didn't have the greatest relationship with them, but I still feel like I'll never be the same, as if they're still here but haven't called me.

Isn't it strange that in death it doesn't always immediately hit us— the reality of it? Of course, most of us feel some instant pain— that empty, cold sadness in the bottom of our gut, but it doesn't actually set in full force until something comes around like your birthday or a holiday. Then it becomes real.

I haven't heard from my family for over a month. Having spoken to my father the day prior to his death leaves me little closure. My mother had been even longer. The last memory I have of her besides her lifeless eyes and splattered blood on the floor of our family home was of my wedding day. She'd chastised me for being lazy, for not getting up earlier, and for wanting to eat and drink. I'd grabbed a sliver of provolone and a cracker off a tray before it was time to exchange vows and she'd slapped it from my hand, telling me not to be fat for the Capo. My job wasn't to eat but to obey.

Obedience was imperative to her, and I was not the type to color inside the lines. I never have been. Luckily, my husband appreciates that piece of me as do the other Vendettis. I was terrified to be left with this family, to be sacrificed as it'd felt like at the time. I had every right to be fearful; however, they've become more of a family to me in a short time than mine ever was. The reality of the revelation is sad, yet freeing, in a sense, because they are my future.

"My birthday isn't until the end of the month," I murmur, gazing over my gorgeous husband. There's no other way to describe him. He's clean-cut, classically handsome, and so powerful the only other word that could possibly fit is Divinity. I won't stroke his ego more by allowing him to know I think such things, even if they are true.

He shrugs, smirking as he watches me crawl from the disheveled bed. His appetite was a bit unwavering last night and he thoroughly used my body. I was sated and snoring before I had time to utter a sleepy good night. Today my body aches in the way a woman's does when she's been loved long and hard.

"Put on a robe and let's have breakfast."

My mouth drops in mock outrage and my hands fly to my cheeks, teasing. "But wait, you don't want me in a business outfit to drink my orange juice? I'm shocked, sir!"

He snorts, tossing me a sleep shirt that says 'spoiled' and my silk robe. "If you'll be calling me sir, then I'll allow it this time." He winks.

Smiling widely, I yank the shirt over my head. Next, I slide on a pair of fluffy, furry slippers and brush my teeth before donning the long, soft obsidian robe. It was another purchase made by my bossy husband without my consent. He has exceptional taste, so it's not much of a hardship having him indulge me a bit.

"We should celebrate the news of this trip." I wiggle my eyebrows, naughty thoughts floating through my mind, and he sighs, grabbing my hand to lead me from the room.

"Trust me, we will, but first I need to let my brothers know immediately so they can prepare. Today I want you laying out anything you'd like to bring along, and I'll have the staff pack it. Go easy, as we'll shop plenty once we're there. The quality and design is exceptionally better than what the States offers, and you'll be able to see the pieces in person."

Rather than reply, I give his hand a little squeeze. I'm becoming more excited about this with each passing moment. Shopping does sound like fun, but I'm more excited to get some time with my husband in another country. Milan flashes into my thoughts, his heated gaze, his forbidden touch...I want him to take me dancing while we're there. I want him to finger me in the middle of the dance floor again, but this time I won't have to leave and fantasize over him. I'll have him.

We're last to make it into the breakfast nook, the various Vendetti brothers sitting in their usual places, leisurely eating. We say our good mornings to each other, and Matteo and I both load plates with various items from the buffet-style foods. This is how breakfast is served every morning, and it's my favorite time to load up on delicious pastries and fresh fruits. My mother must be turning over in her grave with how much sugar I consume first thing in the mornings, but with my husband, I need the energy.

We both sit in our respectful seats, the Capo at the head of the table with me to his side. The brothers gaze at me inquisitively, probably questioning why I'm not dressed properly. They're all freshly showered, clad in expertly tailored suits, mimicking Matteo. I can't believe Romano had them like this every single day of most of their lives. I can't imagine not letting my children be informal to share family meals or run around the house. I hope he doesn't expect me to enforce a dress code all the time. I could understand if it's for dinner or Mass or whatever... but not to eat cereal first thing in the morning. Breakfast should be a time to greet each other and get a good start to the day, not choke through it.

"We're going to Italy," Matteo proclaims, drawing me out of my random thoughts. "I'm taking Violet, Cristiano, Luciano, and Salvatore."

Boom, it's done. He doesn't tiptoe around when it comes to him declaring Vendetti plans or what he wants. Clearly, he's a man used to giving orders and having everyone obey.

Glancing around, I notice Dante and Valentino instantly begin to bristle. Santino keeps his feelings to himself, and I'm a little bit caught off guard. I guess when he told me that we'd be taking a trip, I automatically assumed it would be the entire family. Yes, I want time with Matteo, but I was looking forward to hanging out with everyone and was hoping Dante would finally come around a bit.

"Valentino, you will look after the familia affairs here in the States while I'm out of the country. If anything comes up, you contact me immediately."

Valentino cocks his head to the side. "Me? You wouldn't prefer to contact Romano?"

"No, Romano is retired, and I intend to keep him that way."

"I will do my best and check in with you regularly," Tino answers, and Matteo seems pleased as his gaze falls to Santino.

The Capo turns his full attention on Santino next. "You will help Valentino with anything he may need, as far as the Empire is concerned."

"You have my word," Santino agrees, ever the dutiful soldier. I will miss my friend being around while we're away, but he'll do a good job here. I know Matteo depends on him a lot with the Empire already, so this makes sense.

"Dante," Matteo calls next, and all of our stares lock on the big man in question.

He's been the only one to pull so far away from me. The other brothers haven't skipped a beat much. Valentino was a little weird for a few days, but then he was the same, just less flirty. Dante, however, has been distant and borderline hostile when it comes to me. Matteo keeps saying that it's because he was falling in love with me, and honestly, with more time, I may have been able to fall a little in love with him in return. My husband put a stop to it before my feelings could get that far invested, though, and while I was shocked at his demands when I first heard them, I'm grateful now. He saved my heart from hurting more than it already does from losing Dante's friendship.

"You will go to Chicago to sit at the five familia's monthly gathering to represent the Vendetti familia. We are now a part of that table, and they need to see that we were and still remain serious about holding our place there. Depending on how things progress in that aspect, it may become a frequented trip for you."

"Me?" Dante huffs, brows scrunched.

Matteo nods. "Yes, brother. I know you are strong and can handle yourself amongst anything else there. You need time and space from the Empire, and I'm offering it."

"Fine," he bristles. "You want me gone? I'll go and stay, until you send for me to return."

My husband squints. It's the only tell he shows that he wasn't expecting that reaction out of Dante. Matteo has this ridiculous sense of responsibility when it comes to his family. I had no idea when I first arrived about how much his decisions are based on the whole family, and not just whatever suits him at the moment. I'm sure I still haven't fully grasped his sacrifices.

"Good, I know you will take care of everything in my place," he mutters, but I can easily see that he's not completely sure in what he's saying. Dante was one of the most devoted toward his older brother when I first arrived. Who am I kidding? They all worship him. To witness them at odds has me feeling guilty inside. Did I do this? Are they not on the same page because of me?

"Dante?" I breathe, and his gaze locks on mine momentarily before turning away as if he can't stand the sight of me. I've ruined the protectiveness he used to feel over me; now he can't even look at me. All the while I fall for Matteo a little bit more with each passing day. Dante doesn't have that luxury— another woman to consume his attention and affections. My guilt intensifies the more he suffers, and I wish there was something I could do to make it easier for him.

Matteo continues after a moment of awkward silence. I could kick myself. I should've just remained quiet rather than attempt to offer him some semblance of comfort. I'm a fool. These men aren't used to being coddled when something bothers them. They were taught to suck it up, to grow stronger. I wish I could tell him that it's okay to be upset or angry, that it's a normal emotion, but I know that neither he nor anyone would listen to me speak such words. They don't want to be comforted; they'd rather act like whatever bothers them doesn't exist, or let it fester into anger.

"As for the rest of us, Luciano, you will protect mia fiore while we're away. If I'm not around her, you should be within two feet of her at all times."

Luciano swallows, a bit taken back at being put in charge of my safety. "Yes, Capo, I will guard her with my life if necessary."

"Salvatore and mia fiore will be assisting me with acquiring Cristiano a bride."

Various brothers begin to speak up, stunned with Matteo marrying the youngest off when all of them are far more experienced. They're fiercely protective of the youngest, which is surprising considering Cristiano is no doubt a replicate of Matteo, only younger. He should be raised in his brother's shadow, a perfect fit if, God forbid it, something were to ever happen to the Capo dei capi. Valentino would certainly be next in line. Matteo's shared that tidbit with me, but for the good of the family, Cristiano would be the next best fit. I know it doesn't work that way— that the Capo reins by birthright— but it's still a smart idea when looking out for the prosperity of the Empire.

"Brothers!" Cristiano raises his voice, calling everyone's attention. "Matty isn't marrying me off on his own doing. I have asked him for this. It's my request to be married, to find my future and exchange my vows amongst my devotion to her in the eyes of the Catholic Church."

Santino grumbles, "You'll marry without all of your familia there to celebrate? And what of Romano? Will he be going with you?" His stormy gaze lands on my husband, it's so unlike Santino. He's normally so calm and collected, the easygoing one out of the seven. "Have you even called our father or are you just marrying off his youngest son without his thoughts?"

Again, Cristiano interrupts, "Santino, thank you for your concern. I would like to exchange vows with my bride in the old Italian church by our home there. I was hoping to bring her home, and then get to celebrate my nuptials with my brothers." He's so well spoken and mature, sometimes I forget he's only seventeen and not the second oldest. He and Salvatore should've traded places, no doubt.

Matteo leans back, a blank mask over his elegant features, his high cheekbones reminding me of royalty. "Actually, Romano gave me his blessing on marrying you all off to whomever I see fit. Did you really expect he'd fly to the estate and find each of you brides when the time came?" He scoffs. "He is retired, Santino. I am head of this familia. You all seem to grasp that to a degree, but obviously not the full extent." Matteo steeples his fingers and in that moment looks every bit the Capo dei capi he is. "I'm Boss. If I order you to fuck a hundred whores" –he flicks a glance at Dante before back to Santino— "you will fuck every one of them. If I demand you slit twenty throats, you will, wearing a pleased grin. And so help me, if you disobey me, I will punish you as I see fit. Don't ever forget that you're sixth in the food chain around here."

Santino swallows. His face is a bit pale after angering the powerful man at the head of the table.

"Mia fiore, come here."

At his order, I tuck my napkin under the edge of my plate, taking a quick drink of orange juice and climb to my feet. Pushing my chair in, I make my way to him. I'm not the one questioning or arguing with him; however, my muscles tighten with each step, wondering why he would be calling me to him, when I literally sit in the next chair, a foot or two away. It takes me two small paces and I'm next to his elbow.

"Carina," he murmurs, and my body relaxes with that one word.

"Matteo?" I breathe, and his arm wraps around my waist.

His free hand tugs the tie of my robe free. The silk parts and he meets my curious gaze. "Sit on my lap, precious flower."

He continues to pull me to him, until my hands fall to his shoulders and I have no choice but to straddle his strong thighs, my lips so near his. I could move a few inches and press mine to his. His muscular arm braces me in the spot as his free hand reaches between us. I'm momentarily mute, sitting and waiting before I glance down to notice he's unclasped and unzipped his slacks. He shifts his hips and tugs the opening a bit, holding me firm until his cock is free.

"Matteo!" I gasp with wide eyes. He hasn't had me in front of his brothers in a month's time and I've grown used to our privacy. Not that I don't enjoy the other men's attention on us, because I do. It turns me on quite a bit, if I'm honest with myself.

He smirks, fingers shifting my panties to the side. The head of his thick cock nudges my entrance, making me instantly grow wet. I've had his dick inside me every day this past month and it's left me craving him, after the pleasure he's given me repeatedly.

His arm moves me just a touch until my hips begin rocking a pleasure-driven rhythm on their own accord. My pelvis tilts forward then backward, riding his tip, slowly scooting inch by inch down his long length. Growing impatient, he yanks me to him, seating his length in me to the hilt. With a pleased moan, I attempt to bite back the desire lacing my voice and tuck my face into his neck, breathing in his delicious scent. He reminds me of everything refined and expensive, like a tantalizing aged wine that fulfills all taste buds. Sweet, yet tart and cocky all rolled up together to have me panting for more.

He takes advantage of me tucked so closely to his big frame and leans his chin on my shoulder, watching how his brothers react while rocking my clit against him. I'm so screwed, literally and figuratively. Matteo does not mess around when it comes to fucking. He gives it deep and often times rough, the way I've come to desire the most. "You're soaked, mia fiore, dripping all over my heavy cock," he comments, and I hear a chair scrape.

Dante huffs as he storms out, "Unbelievable."

Matteo holds firm, keeping me in place as he continues to grind me against him. My pussy weeps in pleasure, dripping all over him—needy. "You're not moving until I feel you squeeze my cock as you come," he demands, and like a switch, I shudder. You'd think he reached down and tweaked my clit. He didn't even touch me. His bossy-ass mouth can merely speak and have me nearly orgasm.

"Matteo," I moan and overhear an answering groan somewhere behind me. It sounded like Valentino, but I'm not completely sure. As much as I love being the center of their attention, I can't help but worry that we shouldn't be doing this here. I feel like we've all moved on from the original arrangement and he's just teasing them. *Look at what's mine. Look, but you can't ever touch.* It's a dangerous game; I know this from Alessandro's twisted obsession with finally being with me. That never would've happened with my father alive, nor would I have allowed it.

The cool air hits my ass cheek and I realize my husband has lifted the tail of my sleep shirt, allowing his brothers to see to tops of my globes, clad in underwear of course, but still.

Valentino mutters, "Jesus, Matteo, at least put her on the table so we can see a bit of her pussy."

He growls deep, the sensation vibrating me everywhere, and it's enough to make my pussy clench, throbbing, sucking, milking his cock for every centimeter possible as my orgasm hits me like a truck. I try to hold back, but it's no use. The naughtiness of this morning along with knowing that five men watch me get fucked has me screaming in pleasure into Matteo's neck. The feelings slide over me like a fuzzy, warm blanket. The bliss and comfort mixing with the male scent of my husband, his cologne, and our mixed arousal has my eyes drooping, feeling nearly drugged.

He thrusts upward, holding my hips in place, and I whimper. My pussy's sensitive, miniature sparks of my receding orgasm zapping me with the reminder that I came hard and could take more. At my pleased sounds breathed against his neck, he grips me with a bruising touch, his cock throbbing as he pumps me full of his seed. He made me promise myself to him and ever since, he's taken full advantage of it. He wants me pregnant with his son immediately and has been filling me with his come again and again until I'm too sore to move and have to soak in a bath some days.

"Mine," he proclaims to the rest of the room. The silence surrounding us is stark, to the point I could nearly believe that we're completely alone, when in fact that's not the case at all. "My wife, my woman, *mine*," he declares, the words weighted heavily with their true meaning. It remains noiseless until Matteo is finished filling me of his essence and pulls his cock free, moving to fix my panties back in place. I pull my face from his neck and notice the brothers wordlessly leaving the room.

Once we're alone, I lean my cheek on his shoulder, his still hard, wet cock lying against my thigh. "That escalated quickly. Are you certain it was necessary? Want to share with me what just happened?"

He pulls my hand from his shoulder, bringing it to his mouth, and kisses my fingers. "I think it's time I buy you another ring."

"Matteo, don't attempt to distract me with shiny things. Please talk to me about this."

His mouth breaks into a rare smile, his eyes meeting mine. His irises seem a bit brighter, and I just want to snuggle the gorgeous man. "I was letting them know that I'm serious. That even though some time has passed, I won't be sharing you. It was also a test."

"What sort of test, because I'm thinking you got an A."

He chuckles. "I wasn't being graded, although I do enjoy hearing you'd give me an A. I was testing my brothers. I had to witness their reactions firsthand to me fucking you in front of them."

"From the groans, I'd say they enjoyed it."

He agrees, "Yes, very much so. I was curious to see if my brothers had moved past everything, the lingering emotions from the tradition. Dante is still touchy, but I have a feeling with time he will be back to his usual brooding self. The others were amused, and yes, aroused, but not jealous."

"So that's good then, right? What about you saying '*mine?*'"

"Indeed, mia Violetta. The ending words, well, it was me issuing a warning that if anyone so much as touches what belongs to me without prior permission, no matter who the hell they may be, I will kill them."

I swallow, the action feeling a bit scratchy. I'd say the proclamation coming from Matteo is pretty freaking close to him admitting he loves me.

Matteo 'Ruthless' Vendetti has finally fallen. Who knew it would be to his tiny queen?

Chapter 12

I sailed seas of emotion,

to wander a forest of scars,

I am a dance of light and darkness,

a galaxy of shadow and stars.

- R. Queen

Matteo

Six days in Italy and my little flower has a tan that brings out her Italian heritage. She's even more stunning, and I cannot wait to bear witness to her aging as we spend our life together. I know it won't always be easy; she's headstrong and defiant and definitely isn't afraid to speak her mind. Those are all attributes that grated on me in the beginning, but I'm coming to admire them. They show a sense of her strength. Her long, dark locks shine as the sun beams down on her, casting her in a light that has me swearing she's an angel to my darkness.

"Mia bella fiore," I croon, completely smitten.

She smiles, popping up on her toes to kiss my cheek. Things have been comfortable, even good between us, if I had to say so. I'm not so sure if fucking her in front of my brothers last week was the right idea, but I couldn't help myself. I'm spoiled when it comes to her, and she's fully aware of that. I don't mind sacrificing so much for mia familia, but she's not something I'll give up or share anytime soon.

She spins in a circle, her teal dress flowing around her. She's never appeared more beautiful or free to me than in this moment. She giggles, and I find myself beaming down at her. "What is it?" I ask. "What has you so happy today?" Her mood is infectious, having my chest nearly bursting being near her when she's like this.

"I'm excited about the party tonight," she confesses as I wrap my arms around her and pull her to my chest. I can never be close enough, something I'm learning to embrace rather than curse.

She's broken me in over the last thirty days. I'd never been this affectionate with a woman, but Violet is different. I attempted to resist in the beginning, but every day I've woken up with her sleeping on top of my body, straddling her legs over mine. It's hard not to want to hold her when I've grown accustomed to her small, warm body. I'm still not the lovey type, especially in public, but I do find myself reaching for her more and more.

"Mm, you're excited to wear the new dress we picked out yesterday whilst shopping? I'm looking forward to seeing you in it again."

"Well, yes, but that's not all."

"So tell me."

"Oh no, I have to go get ready, and I'll talk to you later."

"Tease," I murmur, stealing her mouth for a quick, hard kiss. When I release her, I manage to swat her ass before she's out of my reach, and she takes off laughing. The sound of it has me smiling to myself. She's a troublemaker having me feel years younger. Growing up with Romano, you age quickly, and Violet has those taxing years turning backward.

Pulling my phone free, I barely suppress the groan from escaping when I see Romano's name flash on the screen. *Speak of the devil himself.*

"Si?" I answer straightaway.

"Matteo, my sources tell me you are in Italy for Cristiano. I'm on my way."

"You are?"

"Si, he is my son. I want to be there when he marries."

He's full of it; he doesn't care about Cristiano's impending nuptials. He's never been concerned with us personally. It's one of the main reasons why Cristiano is beheld as more of my own son rather than Romano's. "You and I both know that isn't the case. What is the real reason?"

"I have business."

"Hm,"

"I want to meet with the girl's grandfather before you decide on anything."

"Nonsense, I'm the Capo now. You've been away for two months. Things are going smooth and now's not the time to interfere."

"I can certainly see that things have changed. You'd have never spoken to me with such disrespect in the past."

"You'd have beaten me. I do the whipping and dole out the punishments now. I'm not being disrespectful; I'm upfront as I'm Capo dei capi."

"Si," he sighs. "I believe the old-timer will attempt to take advantage of you."

"And what is so wrong with that if I'm aware, if I allow it to happen, and if Cristiano is happy?"

"You would knowingly be taken advantage of, Matteo?" This time he scoffs. "You've already grown soft. Is it that Bottaro *bitch*?" he hisses. "Has she broken *Ruthless* already?"

His words have visions of cutting his tongue out of his mouth assaulting me. "You will not speak of my wife that way. I'm not soft in the slightest, *Romano*, and it would do you and everyone else good to never forget that. If you show up here, you will not speak on my business, and I mean under no circumstance. You want to be here, you come here strictly for Cristiano and his happiness. This is what he wants, and he deserves your support for this at least."

"If you insist then I may come for a time. I doubt I will make it while you're there, however. I may catch you for a day or so."

I want so badly to roll my eyes, but that's not an emotion I readily show, and knowing Romano, he'd be able to see it through the damn phone. Rather than allow myself that one bit of rebellion or to tell the retired Capo off, I bite my cheek. It's had many slices and marks put into it in the past, but the habit's served me well. A coppery tang of blood hits my tongue and I swallow. "Very well. I won't say anything to my brother then, in case you miss it. I know if you make it here in time he will be pleasantly surprised. Oh and how did you discover we were in Italy?"

"I spoke to one of the men to check how things were going for you. I was worried for my sons."

It's complete rubbish. I know it and so does he. I'll have to scold Angelo. While his misplaced loyalty is endearing, it's also infuriating as his loyalty now belongs to me, not my father. I'm also aware that my father was worried about the Empire. His concern has nothing to do with his blood, as long as the money keeps coming in and our familia's name is at the top.

"Right, I have a prior engagement," I mutter, ready to hang up on him before I do decide to remove his or anyone else's tongue.

"Be safe and always remember we reign because of blood. Always protect your familia."

"Good-bye," I return and hang up.

Who in the hell does he think he is with that bullshit reminder. I am the head of this familia. I'm its greatest protector, and I'll be its fiercest leader as well. He can believe whatever he wants, but it's none of his business any longer. He can try to play Capo from the Hamptons, but it won't get him very far. He seems to have forgotten his own life lesson he'd taught me: never underestimate your enemy. With him no longer residing at the head of the table, he's quickly taking the place of enemy.

Pocketing the phone, I make my way to prepare for the party. This little tart better fall over and bow at my baby brother's feet, as I'm not in the mood to be fucked with after speaking to Romano Vendetti.

***

"Luciano will dance with you. I have business to take care of," I tell my beautiful wife. Violet looks beyond amazing this evening. She's always stunning, but tonight she's clad in a thin rose-gold gown that drapes over each curve as if it was sewn specifically for her frame. I'd groaned when I initially caught sight of her, knowing I'd have to hold myself back for who knows how long for this stupid party when I wanted nothing more than to peel the material back off and ravish her thoroughly.

Meeting his stare, I order, "Spoil her. Whatever she wants— champagne, chocolates, dancing...just make sure she enjoys herself."

His lips tilt up as he nods and offers his palm to my wife.

"Behave, carina. Don't make me spank you or tie you up later," I murmur and kiss my wife next to her ear, inhaling the Burberry *'Her' scent* I'd witnessed her dab behind her lobe before we left. She smells light, flowery and feminine. It only makes me desire her even more.

She grins, patting my chest, and teases, "Promises, Matteo. You know a Vendetti always keeps a deal." She winks and places her hand in my brother's. They stroll toward the opulent dessert display before I have a chance to remark on her cheeky boldness. It makes my dick hard. I want to fuck her on all that damn chocolate.

"Matty?" Cristiano draws me from my lustful thoughts.

"Cris, let us go meet this girl, shall we?"

He nods with his irises shining, full of excitement. "Have you seen her yet?" His hands move to check his hair for the twentieth time since he got in the car earlier. It's slicked back, not a strand out of place. Next, they move to his tie. He's anxious, and it makes me eager for him, to see him so pleased about something I'm arranging for him.

"Yes."

I had insisted when I met with her grandfather earlier in the week. No one knows about that, however, except for me. The familia believes this is the first time we're gathering and that we're guests at a party. Truth is, I'd spoken to the old man who was more than pleased to offer his granddaughter's hand up for a Vendetti son's in return.

We're here tonight to make sure Cristiano is content with her before we make a formal announcement to the public and decide on whether they will have a lengthy engagement or not. The old familias are more traditional over here in the same sense as the Vendetti's are. We may have our own traditions, as I'm sure many others do as well, but most American familias would balk at my proposal, unless they'd been raised in the mafia lifestyle. Here I can offer for a woman's hand. Being well-off and from an old familia myself, it would be taken seriously and graciously. I have no clue what my father believed he could accomplish by coming for a visit to talk business, but I don't need him meddling in our decisions.

"She's young but beautiful. You will be pleased," I divulge.

He grins, blowing out a tense breath, eager yet attempting to rein it in. I'm glad he can be excited about this. Anything I can do to make my brothers' lives fulfilling and easier. I have Violet now, and I want them to have wives for themselves. I wasn't really sure what to expect being married but have learned that having a wife really does make you stronger.

I always thought when Romano said to marry as to not come off as weak, that he meant you wouldn't be so tempted by a woman. I was foolish, because marrying the right woman does in fact make you stronger I won't make that mistake again, and my brothers deserve to have what I have. I thought I could share Violet without a second thought, but with each passing day, I grow more possessive. Even now that she is only mine, I find myself wanting to bare my teeth or gun to every male that glances her way. She's mine, only mine.

We take the magnificent red-carpeted staircase to the second floor. The architecture in this old mansion screams money and talent. Its opulence is similar in many ways to our own place about forty minutes from here. Although we no longer throw outlandish parties such as tonight. We haven't celebrated there much since my mother used to visit when we were children.

Giuseppe, Sofia's grandfather, and I prearranged their initial meeting place and chose this specific floor so my brother could escort his possible betrothed down the staircase to the dance floor. I want them to have proper time to meet and see how their chemistry plays off.

"Right in here, Cristiano." I gesture toward a sitting room off to the right of the various hallways. It's decorated in rustic Italian colors of plums, beige, and orange. This room reminds me of Liliana. I know she would've hosted tea or whatever in a room adorned similar to this. I wish our brother had gotten to know her as I did, no matter how short the time was.

We enter and I hear him draw in a quick breath. "Sofia," he hums, stunned.

I glance to him, puzzled. "You know her?"

Cristiano and Sofia nod in unison, smiling. "Sofia is Arianna's cousin," he supplies, and I still have no clue.

"Who?"

His smile breaks as he glances from Sofia back to me. "The florist's daughter, Matty," he shares.

Swallowing my curse, I store the information away, just in case I need to look into this person that my little brother so easily calls 'friend.' I don't enjoy the fact that she keeps being brought up. "Well, greet her properly, Cristiano," I finally order, and the two step to each other, her hands fit into his, and they smile excitedly at each other.

I nod to Giuseppe and he returns it. "Since you know one another, shall we join everyone?" he asks in Italian, and I'm glad Violet is off with Luciano. I'd hate for her to feel uncomfortable because she doesn't understand what's being said. I've been teaching her some, but she's far from fluent.

The old man steps to my side as Cristiano and Sofia stroll arm in arm a few paces ahead of us. This meeting is to be chaperoned as her grandfather requested. Not that I have to worry. I know Cristiano is saving himself for his bride, but I still humored the man. It is proper, after all, to make sure everything goes well on their first meeting; it'll help us come to an agreement. If this is any indication, however, I have a feeling this will be decided and put into play before we leave to go home tonight.

The night passes fairly quickly, though not as swiftly as it would've had my wife been wrapped in my arms. It reminded me of Cristiano's birthday celebration and how I'd been nearly feral in my possessiveness with her around many so-called business associates and low-lying enemies. Over the years under my father, I learned almost immediately not to trust many in the underground crime world. No one has a good motive. They're there to benefit themselves and no other. It's hard for me to turn that off in instances like

157

tonight. These people aren't here to be a threat— I contacted them. Having Violet and Cristiano with me, however, has me on guard even more. Thankfully, Luciano and my men have been watching, so we can attempt to enjoy ourselves.

"I will say it again, Capo Vendetti, my granddaughter would make a smart match for the young Vendetti." Always my last name. He uses it frequently, as if it's a reminder to him just how much merit my name holds and he can't seem to say it enough. "My offer is still in place: fifty thousand and her hand."

That amount of money is pocket change to the both of us, and he's well aware of the fact. In return he gets to reap the benefits of being tied to our name. Many of his enemies will shrink back further upon discovering he's linked to the Empire. On the upside, our roots to this land will deepen. This was where my mother and father were born, myself and my brothers have also been birthed in Italy to have a strong connection to our heritage. When my own bambinos are close to being born, they too will be brought back to our Italian home. Here, our familia is safer, and we need that peace of mind when we're at a vulnerable state. I have to discuss this with mia fiore; she needs to be aware that she won't be at some random hospital near the Empire. Anyone could get to her and our bambino there. I won't have it.

Watching Cristiano make Sofia smile and watching Giuseppe witness it as well has me confidently countering, "Two million dollars and she will be a content wife. You see how my brother has her beaming already. It is a good pairing."

Not that I should even counter in the first place. I'm fucking Ruthless Matteo Vendetti. If I want Cristiano to have the girl, he will, no matter who says differently. Mia bella Violetta must have me enraptured to be so even tempered and willing to bargain when he's receiving the better deal out of it business wise. My pockets and influence run deep enough; I could simply take the girl for my brother and be done with it all.

He turns to me, eyes milky with age yet intelligence shining in them all the same. Holding his hand out, he offers a friendly grin. "You have a deal, Capo."

In return, I shake his hand and offer an easy nod, acknowledging his continued respect. To him I most likely seem to be a foreigner from the States, young, demanding, and inexperienced in my own life. I commend him for presenting me with the respect my title and familia has earned. With this agreement, he in turn should also come to respect me as a businessman. I never do anything without coming out on top.

Chapter 13

No great mind has ever existed

without a touch of madness.

- Aristotle

Violet

"I'm pregnant," I confess to Matteo as soon as I see him.

The party had worn me out and I was asleep in the car before the driver had left the driveway to take us back to the aged Italian mansion we'd been staying at. I'd wanted to inform Matteo of my news before we went out, but I couldn't work up the nerve. I was excited— am excited— but I didn't want the night to take away from my discovery. Knowing Matteo, we wouldn't have gone to meet Cristiano's betrothed. I didn't want to ruin Cris' night when I'd been hearing since before we'd arrived in this beautiful country about how eager he was. It's hard to think of him only two, almost three years younger than myself. He acts ten years his senior most days, and I've gone through my own share of growing up over the past few months.

Matteo falters, and I can tell he's trying to process my words. It's as if he initially heard me but he's not sure if the words were what I said or rather what he wanted to hear. He swallows, and I stare at him, eagerly awaiting his response. I kept my deal to him, just as

Vendettis always do, according to him. I'm discovering the amount of loyalty and the weight of your given word in this family is beyond anything I'd ever experienced before. I foolishly believed my family was what to be expected, but the Vendettis have opened my eyes to another way of living entirely and I don't mean with opulent wealth.

"Si?" he mumbles, swallowing again, as if the big, bad Capo is fearful of saying it aloud. I've never seen him afraid of anything— not one thing. Even facing off with Alessandro, he didn't blink. He has the spine and strength from a different breed of man, yet I swear he seems a bit shaken with the news of a tiny human.

"A bambino— your bambino," I attempt again, using the word he favors when talking about getting me pregnant. He's been patiently teaching me to speak Italian, though it's a feat I'm nowhere near mastering. I wish I could've shared our good news in Italian; it would've made him proud of me, no doubt. At least our children will be raised to speak it as well; they won't struggle as I do.

He takes a step closer, his huge hand flattening to rest his palm over my stomach. There's no bump yet and there won't be for months, but his reaction is endearing. His other massive palm cups my cheek, his thumb lightly caressing. Leaning in, his lips brush mine, tenderly, lovingly. My Capo is cherishing me, and the tenderness from such a hard man has tears filling my eyes. He whispers against my mouth, "Breathtaking, mia Violetta."

A tear breaks free and all I can do is tilt my head. His dark, sparkling irises meet mine, his gaze intense as he murmurs, "You have made me a very pleased man. Grazie." His fingers carefully wipe my tears away.

My mouth seeks his out again, wanting him to know he's not alone, that I'm happy and thankful. I never expected I'd take the news this gracefully. Knowing I'll have a child to love and tend to and that the baby will have a family full of men to love and protect it has me brimming with joy. He wraps me into his strong arms. I'd once despised his touch; now it only offers me warmth and safety. Breaking the kiss, he leans his forehead on mine and I confess, "I wanted to tell you yesterday..."

"When did you find out?" He's curious, his face clad with a warm flush of exhilaration. I would do anything to make him this cheerful all the time.

"Only a few days ago." It's been driving me crazy inside to keep it away from him too. I wanted to scream when I initially found out. I knew he would be overjoyed and it's had me in a great mood ever since.

"Did Luciano take you?" His brow wrinkles, not liking the fact that he may not be the first I've shared this important discovery with. He's always jealous and possessive, not that I mind. It actually makes me feel like he cares, that he wants me.

"I snuck the package in when we were shopping, Luciano didn't even notice."

He smirks, pride shining brightly. "You will make a fierce mother, I have no doubts."

"You think you can handle me through pregnancy hormones, labor, and children?"

"Oh, I know I can. If you get too out of control, I can always have a nanny come in to help, and tie you to my desk for a few days. I'd get you right and proper again in no time."

"Only if there are snacks." I grin and he growls, lifting me so my legs wrap around his hips. "We've already discussed this; you know my demands."

"Giving me orders now, hm?"

"I'm the Vendetti queen, Matteo. Who better to order the Capo about?" Two months ago I never would've had the guts to tease him or order him around, but I know Matteo won't hurt me. He was a bit savage in the beginning, but he's warmed considerably since I've stopped sharing a bed with his brothers and made peace with my responsibilities.

A pleased rumble vibrates his chest, his fingers moving to tangle into my hair. He tips my head to the side, biting the space under my earlobe. A whimper leaves me at the zap of sensation the bite sends straight to my pussy.

His voice is gruff with need against the silky flesh of my throat. "I should get you a crown for this pretty head of yours," he suggests as he nuzzles and nips to his desire.

I'm not going to argue. I mean, the least I deserve is a crown after everything I've gone through to reach this point. "I don't want a typical crown," I admit, and his body stiffens a bit as he chuckles, shaking me with his laughter. His head moves away to meet my lustful stare, a bright, beaming smile gracing his perfect mouth. He never smiles like this, and it has me catching my breath, my breasts swelling as I consume every inch of his alpha beauty he hides away from the world with a scowl. "Beautiful Matteo," I comment, and he scoffs.

"I'm a man, love. You are bella." He peppers a kiss to my lips, my nose, and then forehead. "Now, tell me about this crown." He begins undoing the dainty pearl buttons down my fancy dress shirt he'd picked out, while balancing me in one muscular arm.

"Well, I'm thinking it definitely needs some black."

His brow raises, and I relax my arms so he can push my shirt from my shoulders. "You're far too elegant for a black crown."

"Black diamonds? I suggest. "Mixed with clear diamonds and platinum?"

He rules the crime syndicate of a massive city, he's the boss of bosses...I have to wear some black. Besides, I've kind of grown accustomed to being a Vendetti. A little dark inside people is exactly what they need sometimes.

"Only if you'll wear it for me naked."

"It's a deal, and when our daughter is born, we get her photos done in a crown and frilly dresses."

He snorts, releasing me to plop onto the large canopy bed.

"Matteo!" I gasp, not expecting it.

"First off, you never want anything, yet you'll wear a crown that I'll spend hundreds of thousands of dollars on, and now you're saying we'll have a daughter that will have her own crown as well? I think I'll lick your sweet, soaked pussy until you come to your senses. Where's my bratty wife who likes to argue everything with me?"

With my skirt free, he parts my tender flesh. I'm left in only a sheer, white-lace bra. His idea of underwear and mine are clearly not on the same page. He moves my legs over his broad shoulders. Leaning in, he scents me before running his tongue through my entire slit and groaning with delight. The man takes what he wants, no matter my modesty or nervousness at his sexual attention. The part that has me blushing the most is that I love every bit of it— the groans, the licks, the sloppy wet and sucking noises coming from down there. So much so that he doesn't give up his sweet torment until I'm screaming his name, core pulsing with an amazing orgasm.

"We'll be having sons, wife," he comments after I'm in my blissful haze. "As for the crown, I'll buy you seven, one to wear each day I see you naked," he reasons, and I laugh at the absurdity of it all. He's nude in a flash, pausing to fold our clothes into two neat piles. It's one of his quirks, but I don't mind it one bit. Matteo is who he is.

The gorgeous man tumbles onto the giant pillow of a bed next to me, rolling my body to climb over his sturdy frame. He wastes no time pulling my thighs over his hips. Lining my heat up to his shaft, I sink down over his monstrous length. My pussy is utterly soaked, dripping wet from being so turned on and from the blissful assault his mouth provided moments prior.

"Yes," I croon, raking my hands over his chiseled chest.

He's not overly cut up as Dante is. Even Valentino is pretty sculpted. Matteo is the perfect mixture of soft skin and strength. He has the outline where his abs are, but not the lumpy, deep indentions from a full-fledged six-pack like his two younger brothers have. His arms are strong and when he lifts them to rest his head against them, he has muscular balls on his biceps. I think those are my favorite muscles on his entire physique besides his cock. Third would be his legs. He's no doubt done his fair share of running, a habit I've seen him continue each morning around the estate with men posted in nearly every corner it seems. Ever since I took off in an attempt to help my mother, my husband has amped the security up a ridiculous amount.

"You feel good," I moan as his hands cup my swollen, heavy breasts. His fingertips tweak my nipples, easily plucking the stiff peaks until I'm rocking and hopping up and down like a mad woman.

His arms snake around my waist, hands locking together behind my back. Matteo offers me a cocky smirk before rolling over to his knees. He's a show-off. Grabbing under my thighs, he hoists one knee over his shoulder, leaving the other to rest in the crook of his arm then thrusts that sexy V that's quickly becoming another favorite feature of mine. His cock sinks so deeply I have to hold my breath as to not cry out. My body hums with his touch. He groans with the next drive, hitting the spot tucked deep that makes me go wild.

"Oh God, right there!" I scream. "Keep going, Matteo!" He loves when I say his name during sex and let him know what I like. The more vocal I am, the more we both enjoy ourselves.

Rather than increase his tempo, he slows his moves. Lowering my leg off his shoulder, he leans in close, kissing my lips tenderly. He plunges deep, and then retreats at a slow, steady pace. It has me thrumming in an entirely different way than our usual hurried, careless fucking.

He breaks our kiss, murmuring, "You're everything that I want."

His proclamation has me holding him tighter to my body, wanting his heat to cocoon me with his sweet words.

"I've wanted you from the moment our eyes met in Milan," I admit. I put up a fight, hell, I even hated him for a short time, but deep down, I know I've always dreamed of him. I've craved his dominant gaze, his powerful aurora and burning touch. I fought him and yet he took what he wanted claimed me to be his, and there's nothing sexier than a man who isn't scared to go after what he desires. "My Capo," I sigh, and his dick throbs.

"You like it that I rule the Empire? That I am king to the underground in New York? Does it make you wet knowing your husband would kill another for hurting you?" His words are truthful and being said in the throes of our love making have me exploding.

"Yes! Fuck, yes! I love it that you're possessive, that you'll kill for me. I love belonging to you," I give in and yell.

His cock swells, cum bursting like a volcano. Hot, wet lava fills my core, coating the juncture between my thighs. Do I enjoy hearing him speak like that to me? Damn right I do, but my words have just as strong of an effect on him as well. He's craved my submission from day one, and each time I offer even an ounce, it sends him over the edge of ecstasy. My husband needs control, he craves it, and he enjoys it even more when I fight him for it.

With one last grunt, he empties his cock of the remaining creamy seed. There's no need for him to keep his cum inside me anymore as he's achieved his goal. His lips skirt over each full mound of my breasts, raining kisses in his path, moving lower until he lays his head on the mattress next to my stomach. Staring at the smooth surface, he tenderly strokes the skin, left to right, right to left, then repeats again and again. His cum leaks from me, but I don't want to move in this moment, sated and falling in love with every side to my husband. Matteo or Ruthless the Capo dei capi, both own my heart.

His strokes relax me until I'm lulled into a pleased, deep sleep.

Chapter 14

Even a white rose has a black shadow.

- worldbyquotes.com

Matteo

I'd foolishly believed that becoming Capo would be the most sought after accomplishment in my young life. How did I never put children or a wife before that? Maybe because I'd not had either before to experience the true impact of each? I suppose having a wife could've gone either way. I was extremely fortunate to have Violet land by my side. The thought of becoming a father fills me with so much pride, I could burst. Okay maybe not, but my chest damn sure feels that way.

One thing weighs heavily on my mind: how could Romano be so disconnected with all of us? We were raised as soldiers, built to obey, not be his sons. I can't see myself putting my own children through the cruelty I was shown. I understand now that it is exactly what it was. I'm not whining about it. In the end, it made me hard and strong, it got me to the top of the food chain. To be Capo, one must rule the underground ruthlessly, and I have no problem whatsoever in doing that.

What I can't do is force my son to kill at ten years old, when he'll still have the innocence of a child shining through. Will he be taught to kill, to protect himself and survive? Certainly, if anything, my sons will have the best training when it comes to their safety.

The same goes for mia moglie when it comes to her safety. She has the best already by her side, which happens to be my brothers.

Each day is another day spent with a woman I've grown to love and respect. It wasn't easy in the beginning; I'd thought she'd attempt to off me in my sleep. I hadn't planned on becoming ridiculously possessive over a female for the first time in my life or enjoy tormenting her as much as I did. I was too harsh on her, but what was I to expect? I had to push her, to feel her out and test her. Turns out she's one of the most loyal, giving people I've ever met.

I'd been groomed by a man who watched his own wife kill herself. The kicker of her death is that he didn't take a single step toward her to try and stop her. He just watched solemnly as she'd stared at him brokenheartedly, tears soaking her pale, hollow cheeks, and raised the shiny gun to her mouth. Romano never uttered a single word in rebuke either. Part of me wonders if he was hoping she'd pull the trigger.

He was wrecked in the aftermath; the beatings were brutal enough a few of his men took the brunt of them at times to keep him from killing his own children. Angelo was one of them, stepping in for me at a time my father wielded a broken wooden chair leg. Angelo went down with a few bruised ribs, but we both know it would've been the death of me back then. We were so young, tiny little things compared to Romano's height and strength. The mistresses he once flaunted in front of my mother like arm pieces were not so much better off. His sexual appetites always pushed the boundaries, but they evolved, becoming more abusive than pleasurable.

I would never share any of this with my perfect wife. She's been through enough to have my own tainted memories thrust upon her. Luckily, Cristiano was a baby; he doesn't remember any of it. In all honesty, it's probably why Salvatore turned to drugs and alcohol, but can I really blame him for wanting to escape? I wanted to as well, but I was the eldest; I had to protect my brothers. I still do, when they allow it. Valentino was on the cusp. He'd experienced Romano in a rage a few times and was thrown around. Again, the men stepped in to protect Valentino's small, broken body from being crushed by his own father. Thankfully, the haze or anger swarming Romano began to lighten around that time and he was safe from further memories, except when he was punished for not being the perfect soldier. Luciano and Santino were too young. Like Cristiano, they were left in the care of nannies, and in my father's mind they were out of sight, out of mind. It was a blessing in disguise, his lacking of fatherhood, as it kept them away from his wrath and alive.

So you see, I had to become Ruthless Matteo Vendetti. There were six souls counting on me to grow up, to be strong for them and keep them as safe as I could. I had to evolve into a bigger, meaner, stronger version than our father so I could eventually get him away from us. It's another reason why I do my damndest to give my brothers something if it's within my reach. They grew up believing in me, looking to me for guidance. I didn't whip the obedience into their backs like my father had...I earned their respect from every lash I'd taken in their place. For accepting responsibility for every time a shirt wasn't folded correctly or one of my brothers didn't kill their mark quickly enough. I always took the blame and it festered, part of it bad, evil even, growing and churning, building me into my own twisted monster.

I became Romano's most prized son, the one so fucked up, yet shiny in his gaze. The only person he'd leave his empire to. After everything, my brothers deserved to reap the benefits of the Vendetti Empire. It's their birthright along with my own. The occasional car Romano threw our way for birthdays was nothing compared to the daily hell he put us through. The constant mind games alone were exhausting.

Then in walked Violet Bottaro and completely turned the dark world I'd known upside down. I'd set out to defeat her, but it seems she's the one who's done the conquering. I brought her in, promised to build her up and make her stronger, and she's flourished. She not only brings light to my life, but every Vendetti brother. Now with her pregnant, I feel as if our journey is really beginning. She's not only my now, she's my forever, and she's absolutely amazing. I'd believed that I'd break her, make her my plaything. As it turns out, Violet became my queen. She liked my touch of evil; she spun it up, chewed it like a piece of gum, and warmed me from the inside with her affection.

The Vendettis don't own her; she owns us.

***

Cristiano practically preens with excitement as we all line up at the altar. We've practiced this a few times with him, but now is the time that counts. He's young and hopeful with an entire life of possibilities head of him. He'll have a short time in Venice with his new wife, along with security to celebrate. After the week is over, I'll send the jet for them. He and Sofia will come to live on the estate with the rest of us. I've given my word to Giuseppe that I'll keep my eye on them and help guide them when needed. I'm not too sure if I should be the one to do that, but there's no way I'm leaving my youngest brother here with them. He belongs in the Vendetti home, as will his new wife. Violet will have another woman in the house, and Sofia will have a female only a few years her senior to look to for direction.

"I hope I can make her happy," he mutters as tiny drops of sweat begin to dot his brow.

"Relax, Cristiano. She already favors you. Her mother told me that Sophia's had a crush on you for years."

He nods, cheeks flushing. So young and innocent, even amongst all the hellish things he's done and witnessed in his seventeen years.

"I'm proud of you. We all are." I tilt my head toward my other brothers. Once the deal was struck and we'd had a date planned, I made sure my brothers flew in the night before to be here as well. I thought I could do it without them, but I was wrong. This is a familia celebration and they should all be here for it. Cristiano deserves our combined support behind him.

Our brothers agree with variations of a nod, smirk, or muttered wishes of luck. No one ribs him in this moment as the significance runs deep. To exchange nuptials with your betrothed under the house of God, well, it's forever. We're Italian; old-fashioned and Catholic religion is of great importance to many of us. You don't make a promise under the Almighty's roof and not fight tooth and nail keep it.

I can understand Cris' nerves and the bit of sweating. I was edgy when I exchanged my own vows and took on my bride. Of course, I didn't let an ounce of any emotion show. I couldn't. She was a Bottaro, and in the past, they'd always belonged to our list of enemies. I never would've expected for her loyalty to be placed in me among becoming my wife, nor her resilience and strength to take on our entire familia. I'm a lucky man, and I can only hope Cristiano is as blessed as I have been.

172

"Wipe your brow," I order. I'm directly beside him after Violet walked him down the aisle. I was surprised when he requested she do it. His reasoning being that she's his sister was good enough for all of us, and my wife was honored. She wants so badly to tell them of her pregnancy, but we've decided to wait until we're back in the States. She refuses to take away from Cristiano's time here, and I admire her all the more for it. She's the Capo's wife; she has every right to be selfish, yet she doesn't. It only makes it easier for me to offer my cold, black heart to her.

"Am I good?" He flicks his wide gaze to me.

"Si." I straiten his tie again. It's unnecessary, but it'll distract him, and that's exactly what he needs in the moment. A serene melody from a harp floats through the air and I step away, leaving him to see his soon-to-be bride.

"Bella," he whispers in awe, gazing at her as if she's the loveliest young woman in the room.

I look to my own wife, noting her lengthy, dark, silky locks curled and pinned so her elegant neck is on display. Her lips are a shiny peach, long lashes painted with kohl to accent their length, and her ears sparkle with the blush diamonds I'd presented her with this morning. She wears a simple, flowing gown, the lavender showing off her stunning Italian olive-toned skin. My wife loves color, and it suits her. She's so bright and graceful that I can't seem to take in enough of her light to mollify my demented soul.

I should've confessed before we came that I'm in love with her. We're all up here, pretty much sitting ducks; anything could happen to us in a split second. I have men swarming the church inside and out, yet still, I don't approve of her being out of my reaching distance. Sofia comes to stand next to a grinning Cristiano, and our attention's trained on the young couple about to pledge their lives to each other.

The Father begins, leading us with a prayer. "Welcome, brothers and sisters, faithful servants of the Lord." He says it all in Italian. I'd warned Violet ahead of time so she wasn't caught off guard. She's been doing so well learning more words here and there. She can tell me she want's pizza quite fluently, and it brings me more joy than it probably should. Minutes pass, everyone watching the couple and the priest. I'm staring at Violet, so caught in my thoughts of her that it takes a moment for me to realize something has happened.

Blinking, I gaze around as mumbles of outrage, gasps, and shocked faces meet my perusal. Cristiano and Sofia both peer toward the double-door entry. My brother appears panicked, and Sofia's furious. I follow their line of sight until I notice the tear-stained face of another girl their same age. Is that...the florist's daughter?

"Don't do it!" she pleads. "Please, Cristiano! I promised you years ago I would be yours someday and I meant it. Sofia, you're my cousin and I'm sorry, but Cristiano has always possessed my heart," she proclaims with a sob, and my stomach churns. *Fuck.*

Chapter 15

The scariest monsters are the ones

that lurk within our souls...

- Edgar Allan Poe

Matteo

Months pass by, and we haven't returned to Italy since the day at church. We left immediately. I've spoken to Giuseppe and the betrothal is still in place, yet Cristiano has not returned to collect his future wife. I made concessions that he was too distraught in hurting his longtime friend to continue with the ceremony when in truth my brother has no idea what to do. He's too young to deal with this.

I should've made him go through with the wedding— Romano would've. I couldn't do it. One look at him, as if he'd seen a ghost, and I'd yanked him from the church before anyone could protest. He's confessed that he may love Arianna, yet we've already arranged for him to marry Sophia. I've bought him a year's worth of time for him to make peace and allow his heart to move on. I can't do much more than that. He is a man now, one who made his decisions, and he must keep his word.

Dante remains in Chicago, but he seems to be doing better there. The rest of us, however, feel as if a limb has been severed. We're used to having his broody bulk around the estate. He's made an unlikely ally: Thaddaeus Morelli. The man's a Chicago-based gangster that I'd caught wind of growing up. In the underground crime syndicate, it's hard not to hear about various individuals making waves. His uncle is in charge in the area and the knowledge has me wondering if my brother's newfound friend doesn't have an ulterior motive. Dante could rule that city should he desire, and he'd have the Vendetti Empire backing him. He only needs to utter the word, and there will be a war brewing in the windy city as we wipe out the smaller familias.

Valentino enters my office, his angelic features turned into a hard scowl.

"What is it, Tino?" I ask, looking up from the agenda-pushing *New York Times*. The fact that they do the local politicians' bidding makes me sick. Even I had enough sense to turn the former senator and mayors down. He strides to one of the leather high-back chairs and stands, hands braced on the top of the left seat.

"The Irish, they've gone too far."

Sighing, my fingers go to my temples. It's always the Irish or someone of that sort. Being Capo dei capi of New York, I eventually deal with them all at some point. "Si?" These various familias wanted to test the waters, having discovered that I'm ruling the Vendetti Empire and Romano has retired. No one knows where he is; they can't or they would've show up with a bullet to sink into his skull. He has some protection, being rich, but not even a quarter compared to when he was Capo.

"Some prick challenged me at dinner. I was at Chateau' with a date, in the middle of eating dinner, when an Irishman approached me, informing me that he was leading the Irish mob and he was coming for me. The nerve! I'm Valentino fucking Vendetti! Exactly who the fuck does he think he was threatening?"

"Calmati, Valentino," I mutter, brows raised.

He scowls but does as ordered.

"He most likely believed since you are third under Romano that you'd be easy picking. He threatened you, as being under his station. He's unaware that in this familia you were trained more as second; that you are my right hand. He's foolish. Now deal with him swiftly and harshly. Make an example out of him and be done with it."

"Yes, Capo." He smirks, as I've just given him permission to do whatever he wants to.

Salvatore may be the second oldest, but he's too irresponsible to help me run the Empire. I have Violet, but her being pregnant, I don't want her dealing with this sort. She dips her hand in some of our various businesses, learning what she needs to. She's also sat in my place at one of the weekly meetings, so the lesser mob would know she is the Vendetti Queen. I wanted it loud and clear that if something happens to me, my wife will run things and down them all in the process. From what my men and Valentino report, she was well-received.

"Keep me updated."

"You have my word."

I nod, and he leaves as Cristiano approaches from his smaller office. "You wanted to speak to me?"

"I'm going to take Violet to Italy soon. She's getting closer to having the bambino."

"You're still waiting until birth to see if it's a boy or girl?"

With a huff, I agree. It wasn't my idea. Violet insisted. "We all know it will be a son. I think mia moglie enjoys tormenting me far too much by making me wait."

He grins and I continue, "I want you to come with me. You could court Sofia, give yourself time to spend with her before the wedding."

"I can't just yet," he sighs. "I can't stand to hurt Arianna, and that will happen if she sees me with her cousin."

"Sofia is your betrothed, Cristiano, the wedding you asked for and then agreed on."

"I know, and I will go through with it. I just need more time and distance. I want Arianna to have a chance to move on."

"Fine, but you only have two months until your time is up. Use your stretch wisely. Sofia has waited without so much as a passing complaint."

"I know. She's texted me good morning and good night every day since I left, and she has never whined or chewed me out for it."

"Sofia will make a good wife. One who knows her place in all of this," I comment as Severo texts, letting me know the doctor has left. He was doing a weekly checkup on Violet and the latest is to make sure she's okay to travel. He'll be traveling with us just in case the flight induces labor. Women aren't supposed to fly after a certain point, so we're taking more precautions to keep her and the bambino safe. "I need to see mia Violetta."

"Of course," he acknowledges, relieved the conversation is put on hold for now.

***

Violet

"Are you ready to go, mia fiore?" Matteo asks as he glances over the abundance of clothes piled on our bed.

With a huff, I gesture to the absurd amount of belongings. "I have no idea what to bring. I'm the size of a barrel right now. Some things I read tell me I'll be close to this size after mia bambino arrives, and others say I'll lose a lot of the pounds." Pausing, I take a careful bite of the fresh, warm minestrone soup the chef prepared for lunch today. I hadn't been down to bug her for anything so she sent it up, worried I was ill. She also sent tiramisu, but she claims that treat is for the bambino, so it'd be rude not to feed it to him.

They all say I'm having a boy, but I disagree. Every time Matteo lays his head on my tummy, there's a kick, which that alone tells me it's a feisty girl. I need to have a girl; I'm in this huge house surrounded by temperamental, spoiled males. Every single one of them has requested I name the child after them. Well, besides Dante anyhow. I wish he'd come home, but he refuses, so I respect that and leave him alone. I never started this journey meaning to break his heart. Matteo's heart definitely, but not Dante's. In the end, I've hurt one and fallen in love with the other.

"Mia bella fiore, you make everything radiant."

An unladylike snort leaves me as I roll my eyes. He's smooth. Once a pigheaded ass, he's now full of compliments when he's around me. Not that I mind. In fact, I adore him for it. "Thank you." Waddling closer, I hold his biceps for support so I can lean up and kiss his cheek. "I don't understand why it's so important we have the baby in another country. I want to be home, surrounded by our familia."

"It's tradition. Romano, Liliana, myself, and all of my brothers were born there. I want our children to be a part of that tradition. Do this for me?"

Closing my eyes, I inhale and make peace with it. "If it'll set you at ease, then we'll go. I've already agreed."

"But not easily. You've become quite the bargainer," he grumbles, and I smile.

"I've learned from the best."

"Oh no doubt. I'm giving up any say I could've possessed when it comes to the bambino's name."

He wasn't kidding when he mentioned me striking a deal. He wanted the birth in Italy; I wanted the option to pick our child's name. I have no problem if it's a boy to have his middle name be Matteo, but he will not have the exact same name as his father. I don't want him to be a junior and there's no way in hell he'll carry Romano's name or anything close. If it's a girl, I'm naming her Liliana. I haven't shared that bit with anyone as I know it will hit a nerve. I truly believe that if I name her and we bring her home without anyone's knowledge, they'll get to meet this little angel and she can once again bring happiness to such a special name to this familia.

If it's a boy, I had thought of calling him Alessandro, but that would infuriate Matteo after everything with my brother. Not only that, but my brother has pretty much ruined the name for me. There's still time to decide on something. I figure it'll come to me when something fits.

"How are you feeling? The doctor didn't come to my office, so I'm assuming everything was fine?"

"I'm okay. My feet hurt, but considering the boost of energy I've been offered lately, I won't complain. The doctor said I'm good and that the time is getting closer."

He wraps his arms around me, placing a gentle kiss on my forehead. "It's the nesting. You're getting ready for our little one."

I nod and lean into his solid frame. I can never be close enough to him. "Now I need to be thoroughly fucked."

He draws in a sharp breath at my words, and I smile into his chest. I get far too much enjoyment when I catch him off guard. "I can arrange that."

"Oh, good. My pussy started to drip the moment you entered our suite and I could smell your cologne."

He growls, causing my smile to grow wider. "Then waddle that sexy ass to the empty side of the bed so I don't hurt you. It sounds like my tongue needs to lick your pussy first, if you're that wet already."

"Mm," I agree and release him for the clothes-free side. Eagerly, I watch him take piece after piece of his suit off, folding it neatly before removing his white undershirt and plain black boxer briefs. I've learned over time it's the only color he owns. My husband is so simple yet so complex all at the same time. "How can you be so sexy? It's not fair to look like a god when I'm this big."

He smirks, sauntering toward me, heavy, full cock bobbing as he approaches. "If you saw yourself through my eyes, you'd never even question it. You're swollen with my child inside you. There is nothing sexier, mia moglie. Knowing I put that bambino in you and that you will be the mother of our children is the biggest aphrodisiac I've ever experienced. Now lay on the bed and shut up. I only want to hear you when I'm fucking you with my tongue or cock."

I glare, but it's only full of heat, and then do as he says. I'm no longer shy in the least bit, so I spread my legs wide. My pussy on full display drips with wetness for him. Laying my thighs to the side, I order, "Lick my pussy, Matteo. Make me come."

Dropping to his knees, he obeys, tongue eagerly lapping at my core until I'm screaming for him to dip inside me. He's dangerous with his mouth, not only from the commands he can issue from it, but from the pleasure he knows how to inflict as well. "Please," I beg as he draws my clit between his lips, sucking and flicking his tongue until my hips jump.

The only relief he offers is pushing a finger in knuckle deep. My pussy greedily throbs, coaxing him to drive in farther. I need him deeper, wider and harder everywhere. My hormones have already been out of control, nearly borderline insatiable, no matter how many times he fucks me to sleep or utter soreness. Matteo, my hardened, controlling husband refuses to take me as crazily as I often end up begging him to. He's frightened he'll harm me or the bambino, which is ridiculous; I want him to go wild.

"Harder!" I yell, and he growls into my heat, the vibration making me spasm with sensation. "Do it, Matteo!" I yell again, and he stops completely. "Ugh," I groan, and he bites the inside of my thigh. It'll be an interesting addition to discuss when I'm in labor and everyone notices a bite mark next to my pussy. "I was so close."

"You're mouth, mia fiore. If you don't beg me or sugarcoat the words, so help me, I'll gag you if I have to." His threat only serves to turn me on more, and the words automatically poor from my lips. I crave him too badly to just reach down and finger myself until I orgasm. I want his long, fat cock to penetrate me until I clench his steal so tight his face turns red.

"Husband," I breathe, panting from his tongue lashing. I'm right on the edge. "Please, my gorgeous, bossy-ass, perfect husband...please fuck me. I know you're hard and needy. You want this soaked pussy as badly as I want that huge cock."

"Jesus, Mary and Joseph," he mutters, peering up at the ceiling. His blazing irises meet mine. "I don't know what I ever did to deserve you, but I pray every single day to thank the heavens for giving you to me."

See? More sweet words pouring from his mouth. Ever since I became pregnant it was like a switch was flicked and he couldn't cherish me enough. He has his moments, but over the months he's become increasingly more careful on what he says to me and what tone he uses. I don't know if it's because he respects me so much more now than in the beginning or what, but it's made falling in love with him beyond easy.

"I love you, Matteo," I finally admit after months of it being on the very tip of my tongue. Hell, I wanted to tell him two weeks in that I was falling for his stubborn ass, but couldn't work up the nerve. Now it's the opposite: I can't stop thinking about it, especially with him always muttering stuff like he just did.

"Mia Violetta, I know," he replies quietly and adjusts so his cock can fill me. He pushes in to the hilt, making me moan in complete bliss. "So, so breathtaking, mia moglie," he murmurs, swiveling his hips until I whimper because it feels so damn good. I love when he speaks to me in Italian when we're this close. I don't even care what he's saying and oftentimes his purr is too quick for me to catch the words to figure out their meanings. I've gotten better with time, but he could've been reciting definitions from a dictionary for all I know. It doesn't matter; it's his own special aphrodisiac, along with his scent and the way he can move those strong hips and sexy V.

"Yes, my husband, right there."

"Mm," he groans, peppering kisses over my throat, pausing to bite my breasts, and then continue with the kisses where I love them most. He tweaks my nipple in one hand, bracing his upper body off my stomach with the other, and I'm skyrocketing.

"Oh, Matteo, yes! I'm coming," I scream. I'm sure the staff has heard me many times passing through the hallway. They'd never mention it, but I can't help but blush at times, thinking they must be convinced that we're crazy in our play time.

"That's it, fiore, good girl." He swivels his hips again, groaning as his cock swells, on the verge of spouting.

"I want you with me," I beg, as my core clamps around him. My hands fly to his shapely ass and I yank him to me with all my might. I want him buried in my pussy as deep as possible.

His hips jump, rubbing my clit, and second orgasm follows the first, and I'm so worn out, I'm panting, mouth hanging open, watching as he finds his release with my eager pussy. His jaw clenches, teeth gritting as he jerks, cum pumping from his swollen head seated all the way to my womb. He breathes deeply, bracing himself in place as he catches his breath. It was quick and intense and I finally admitted that I love him. I wish he would've said it back, but it takes time for him to come around to feelings...he'll say it when he's ready. Even if he never admits it, I know he feels the same way. I notice it every day in the way he looks at me.

"You're amazing, unbelievably amazing," he says on a powerful exhale, then he's pulling free, taking his warmth with him. "Now that mia queen has had her demands met, let's get you in the shower, and then I'm taking you home."

"We are home, Matteo. This is our home."

"I know, bella, but Italy calls, and you owe me a bambino," he says with a wink and follows it up with a charming grin. Bastardo gets whatever he wants when he gives me that look...

Chapter 16

Unearth

Rare is the soul who holds my heart

- Segovia Amil

Matteo

"Surprise, it's a girl, Capo!" the good doctor cheers, turning to me with this flawless tiny bundle enfolded in fine pink fabric. Ever so carefully, he transfers her into my arms, the world as I'd known it coming to a screeching halt. Her lips move to a pout, and in that very moment I know I'll give her whatever her little heart desires.

She's the first Vendetti Princessa, and she'll rule the world if she wishes. Her papa will make certain of it.

***

Violet

Doting is not a word I'd ever anticipated would come to mind when I thought of my husband, but he is indeed doting. When the doctor had informed us that Liliana was a girl, I was filled with pride. I'd had a girl...I'd known it all along that she'd come kicking and screaming into the world to be by her mommy's side. I won't pretend that I wasn't apprehensive at Matteo's reaction to the news, because I was. He was so set on having lots of sons before we'd even discovered that I was pregnant that it had me a bit anxious. It was all for nothing though. I should've known with how devoted my husband is to the familia that he'd be more than thrilled no matter what with our precious child.

"Her name's Liliana," I share, and he chokes. His eyes grow wide, stunned at the news, appearing as if I'd just kicked him in the stomach. "I don't know much about your mother, but as the former matriarch of the familia, she deserves to be honored. I notice how you all never speak of her, and when I'd brought her up, each of you were overcome with sadness. Whether any of you will ever admit it or not, you all miss your mother. Liliana is going to bring joy to our home and cast light on your mother's memory."

"Mia bella fiore..." he trails off, and my stomach twists, not wanting him to fight me on my decision. He needs to accept this gift. I can't offer many things, but this is one thing I can. He collects himself, sitting on the bed beside me, gazing at our daughter sleeping peacefully in my arms. Reaching forward, he cups my cheek, irises finding mine. "I love you, my wife, more than I could ever express. Thank you for all you've given me."

After all this time, he finally says it aloud, and my eyes fill with joyful tears. Our road hasn't been easy in the least bit, but it was worth every struggle to finally reach this point. Careful so as to not disturb our sleeping Liliana, he presses his lips to mine. His kiss is coaxing, tender and full of so much affection and love. My moody Capo has finally lowered the wall I'd been working hard to climb over for the past eleven-almost-twelve months.

"I love you, too, Matteo," I whisper, happier than I can ever remember being before. He takes Liliana from me, moving her to the bassinet placed beside the bed, and fusses with my pillows to make sure I'm content.

"Sleep, mia moglie. Our princess will wake and want her mama soon. You need your rest; you have the most important job in the Empire." He lies beside me, my head moving to his shoulder rather than the pillows. He's so much more comfortable.

With a smirk, I snort, "The Empire wouldn't run, if it weren't for your obsessive diligence, Matteo. All of us know that and are grateful for all you do for everyone."

"Liliana is the Empire— we all are— but she's the future of it. You're her mother, and while I'll always be there for her and you, it's you, moglie, that will do the bulk of her shaping. She couldn't be luckier to have such a strong mama."

"I'm the fortunate one, Matteo." I press a kiss to the skin of his shoulder, burrowing a bit closer. I can't move around much. My vagina is still on fire after pushing a kicking little girl out of it not too long ago. "So what's next? I know you have a plan."

He chuckles, his voice bringing me comfort, making me feel at home. "Of course, I have a plan. We're Vendettis, carina. We always have a plan."

"Deals, plans...you sound like a Capo," I tease.

"Si. For now, my love, let's just live. We'll worry about everything else tomorrow. I have everything I want right here in this moment."

<u>Epilogue Part 1</u>

I will destroy you in the most beautiful way

possible and when I leave, you will finally

understand why storms are named after people.

- phuckyoquote

Violet

8 years later...

"What are you doing, mommy?" the nosey little girl at my side asks as she peers over the piles of paperwork on my desk.

"I'm working."

"Why are you working?" she queries, cocking her eyebrow, mimicking her father.

"Because, Papa had to go on a trip and he needs my help."

"Not just a pretty face," she proclaims with a wink. Again, exactly like her father. He likes to remind me all the time that I'm more than a beautiful woman on his arm. "Uncle Danteeeee has a girlfriend!" she singsongs, catching my attention.

"What? How do you know this?"

Her silly giggle floats through the room as she dances around my office. She loves it that she's said something to get my attention away from the papers spread out in front of me. Her long hair bounces wildly with her little pixie body.

"Lili! I asked you a question."

With a huff, she slowly walks back to the desk. With one foot in front of the other, she acts like I'm about to shove broccoli down her throat. "Fiiine," she drones, plopping into the seat across from me.

She's eight...EIGHT years old, and being surrounded by uncles, she's downright spoiled rotten. They don't get the rotten side though. I do. "Speak, child. How do you know Uncle Dante has a girlfriend?"

Her little shoulders bounce, eyes sparkling so much like the uncle she's talking about. "I kinda took his picture he had in his room. I'm going to give it to you straight, ma, she looks a lot like you."

Releasing a breath, I pray to Mother Mary for patience. She had a child, so I'm sure she understands better than anyone up there. "First off, don't call me 'ma'; we discussed this. I don't care if you're Italian through and through, you don't get to call me 'ma' until I'm at least forty. Secondly, what do you mean you took it?"

Her finger taps against her chin before her clever gaze meets mine and she smiles devilishly. "I'm a Vendetti. I take what I want."

"Christ," I murmur. She's been around those men far too much lately. She'll be ruling the world by the time she's twelve, if I'm not careful.

"You don't take anything that doesn't belong to you, Lili. It's wrong, and you'll be punished if I find out it happens again."

Her brow rises, unused to me threatening her. She's a papa's girl all the way, and Matteo swears she does no wrong.

"Mr. Cuddles, that new kitten Uncle Santino brought you, will go to the staff house."

Her mouth drops open, bottom lip beginning to wobble. She's good, I'll give her that, but with her father and me, what can I expect. "But, Mommy!" she gasps dramatically, and I hold my hand up. Her mouth snaps closed, ready to be obedient suddenly.

"Where's the picture?"

She opens the Coach cross-body purse she wears daily, roots around for a second, and hands over the small photo. It looks like it was a regular printed four-by-six photograph but cut down smaller. Lili sets it on the desk and slides it closer so I can pick it up.

It's me. Not just any picture, it's from nine years ago when I'd first come to the Vendetti estate. I swallow, my throat feeling tight and dry, my blouse constricting. This was from another lifetime it seems. Nine years and Dante never married, never brought a girlfriend or date around...He barely comes home to this day. I thought he'd come home soon after he was sent to Chicago, but that wasn't the case at all. I barely saw him again after he left. Birthdays, Christmases, and weddings I'm able to catch a glimpse of his bulky, brooding frame. He'll even flash me a friendly smile, but it's impersonal, two strangers passing in a hall. In reality, that was never the case at all. He loved me and I could've loved him too had he stuck around, had Matteo not claimed me for himself once and for all.

"Mommy why do you look sad? She's pretty, like you."

Blinking, I flash her a smile and rein my emotions in. I store the photo away in one of my drawers; I can visit it again sometime when I have a moment alone. Those memories are not suitable for right now.

"Yes, indeed. Let's keep this between us. We don't want to upset Uncle Dante or have his brothers tease him. He had it in his room for a reason. Okay?"

She nods, totally innocent, and I'm taking advantage of that, but I can't dig up old graves at this point in my life. There's a commotion, like running coming down the hallway, garnering our attention.

"Ma!" my six-year-old son yells as he storms into the room. "Will you tell Uncle Luc I can have snacks?"

"Ma," I mutter, shaking my head. *These damn kids.*

His little brother comes racing in behind him— he's fast for four. They remind me so much of Luciano and Santino, being close in age and thick as thieves. "Mama!" He grins excitedly and runs my way.

Holding my arms open, he runs straight in to give me a bear hug. I sniff his hair, as he holds me tightly. My little guy is adorable. All of my children are cute but terrors.

He leans back and pokes my stomach, "Mama you getting big!"

With a groan I let him go and lean back. "I'm not big; I have your little brother growing in there. Mia bambino."

He snorts, eyeing me like I'm crazy. Luciano rounds the corner and I shoot him a death glare. "Working, remember?" I told him I could take on the princess if he kept the other two occupied.

"My bad, babe. Smartass One and Two said they could have cake. I told them they had to ask you first so you didn't kill me later for feeding it to them."

"Cake, Matty?" I ask my six-year-old and he shrugs, and then puffs up his small chest.

"It is my favorite snack," he admits, and I can't help but smile.

"Fine." My hands go up in surrender. "They can have cake, but afterwards, they need to play kickball or something."

Luciano nods, understanding I want them to run some of the sugar off before I'm back on mom duty. "You got it."

"Oh yeah! Caaaaake! Let's go, fella's," Matty screams and runs out of the office, and the other two follow yelling cake. It's Luciano's turn to glare, but I know he really doesn't mind, and the kids adore their uncles.

Angelo pokes his head in. "Heya, Mrs. Vendetti?"

"Si, Angelo?"

"That meeting I spoke to you about earlier, with the Russians?"

"Si?"

"They've arrived. Are you sure about this with the Capo gone? I could have them come back if you'd prefer."

"Nonsense, I appreciate that they felt comfortable contacting us on their unplanned trip. Please, send them in."

He nods, relaying the message for Luigi to go fetch them. He comes to stand behind and off to my left side. He's good about always watching my back when Matteo's not around.

"Grazie, Angelo," I acknowledge, and he tips his head in my direction then lowers his gaze in respect.

I hit a button under my desk, letting Santino know he's needed. He uses the office two doors down; my husband likes to keep me surrounded with protection and help.

"Carina?" Santino greets seconds after.

"I'd like you to sit in on this meeting. I don't need you to intercede, just your presence."

"Of course. You want me here?" He gestures to the seat in front of my desk.

"No, please sit to my right."

His gaze widens slightly, taking in Angelo's spot, then drags an extra chair off behind me to my right. It's exactly how Matteo would sit if he were having a similar meeting. The fact that no one questions me on it and just does what I ask shows a lot in how much they respect me and my position as matriarch of the familia.

Tall, well-built, handsome men enter— only two as no more would be permitted to be this close to me without my husband by my side. "Mrs. Vendetti, it's a pleasure," the one in front immediately greets, voice heavily laden with a Russian undertone.

"Mr. Mikhailov." I stand, holding my hand out to properly greet him. He's an extremely dangerous, powerful man in Russia.

He flashes a kind smile and takes my hand in his. "I do not wish to disrespect the Capo dei capi and kiss your hand. Please my intentions are respectful."

I return his smile. "I understand, and grazie for it."

He nods, releasing my hand to gesture to the man beside him. "Moy Brat."

"Hello," I greet his brother and hold my hand out to him next in respect. I'm assuming this must be his right-hand man for him to feel the need to introduce him as well. I gesture to Santino. "This is the sixth Vendetti." It's how I was taught to announce Matteo's brothers when we're in this situation.

The Russians' gazes both lighten at getting to meet one of the infamous Vendettis, though I'm quite known now as well.

"Please, sit. Would you care for a beverage?"

"No, we are fine. This trip, it was...unexpected. Younger brat." He shrugs like 'younger brother' explains everything. Being around all of the Vendetti brothers, I can empathize.

"Shall we get to the point of this meeting then?"

His head tilts. "I have heard you have princess. I came to offer moy sin."

"A betrothal? You are aware my daughter is only eight years old?"

"Da," he agrees. "Moy sin is ten."

"And you'd like to arrange something already?"

His head tilts side to side before admitting, "I was hopeful. Is it too soon? Have you not been offered?"

This man is obviously used to his own language, and me mostly speaking Italian has this conversation coming off a touch choppy. I've studied other languages over the years around my husband, though, so I can understand many. I can't speak them, but I have a decent idea of what others are saying at least. Matteo surprised me when I found out he could speak four languages fluently. I should've expected it, though, with how tedious and smart he is.

"On the contrary, Mr. Mikhailov, you are the fifth to ask for my daughter's hand."

Another thing that had shocked me, Liliana's first marriage offer came in when she was four months old. I was livid; Matteo and his brothers were preening with pride. They said it was a good thing. I was still pissed. Over eight years, I've made peace with it, but with how much control I possess, I'm in the position to make sure she has a wonderful husband. This is our life, the mafia; we arrange our children's marriages all in the name of money and power. Are we monsters? Probably, but at least I love my children enough to make sure they get the best. I will never treat them as my own mother had with me.

"Fifth! Nyet... I am too late?"

"No, we're actually waiting to accept an offer just yet." He smiles and I continue. "If we were to agree, when would you want them to marry?"

"Fifteen?" he asks, and I shake my head.

"Nineteen at the earliest," I easily disagree. "And would there be a courting period? I don't want my daughter going into a marriage blind."

"That can be arranged, I can have moy sin come and stay with you or your princessa is welcome at moy home. Moy wife would love another female to speak to."

I doubt that very much, but I keep my opinions to myself. "That is a very generous offer. Is there anything else on the table?" Normally, this is where I'd be offering them land, money, drugs, weapons, or something in that matter being that I'm the one with the daughter. His son will be expected to take care of her for the rest of her life. In this case, however, we are Vendettis; we have the upper hand from our name alone. The offers for Liliana, I've discovered, come with promises of many various luxuries.

"I can give you a chain of hotels I have here in America." He glances at me, taking in my looks. I know I'm beautiful. I've been told almost every day of my life for the past nine years from Matteo or someone in this house how stunning I look, and I can see it in the Russian's eyes he believes so as well. He's probably thinking that my daughter will be just as striking. Little does he know, she far surpasses me. "Or perhaps raw jewels? Diamonds?"

Beauty and power to the Russians is a gold mine. I have no doubt they'd agree to whatever I have in mind. At his last addition, I smile. "That is very generous. I would like to meet your son sometime if possible, and I'd like you to meet Mr. Vendetti. I have a feeling we may have a very prominent future ahead of us."

He beams, standing quickly enough that I know it has Angelo twitching with anxiety, ready to pull his glock free and unload two into the head of the Bratva. Mimicking him, he takes note of my protruding stomach.

"I shall have my wife pregnant." He nods like it's the best plan ever.

My hand rests on my tummy protectively and I chuckle. "Unless you have girls? I seem to only have boys, besides my oldest daughter." Not that Matteo would marry two of our children off to the same familia. Well, unless his plan was for our children to overrun the other familia completely, but that could get a bit too dangerous than I'd be on board with when it comes to mia bambinos.

"I will leave you to rest. It was much pleasure to discuss our children's futures. I will look forward to meeting with the Capo."

"Thank you. If you are back in New York, perhaps we can have dinner and talk again?" I offer, and he wisely accepts and bids his good-byes. The meeting was quicker and easier than I'd been anticipating with my husband not here by my side.

197

The room clears and Santino presses a kiss to my forehead. "You make us proud every day. It's an honor to have you at head of the familia."

I hug him in response, his approval meaning a lot.

They often tell me I'm doing a good job, but being a scatterbrained mom at times makes it hard to believe. Mama is no doubt the most important role I have here, but then there is also the wife, queen, and Vendetti role as well that I have to fill. It can be overwhelming, but so far I've managed to get through it. Matteo's continued to push me throughout the years and because of him, I've thrived. I couldn't thank him or love him enough for everything he's given me, not just the material possessions, but my children and his unwavering love and loyalty.

"You're only proud because I didn't shoot this one," I comment, and he smirks.

"That too. I think you had Angelo on edge. The poor guy is tired of cleaning up your bloody messes."

I snort. "Even Matteo would've shot the last idiot that questioned my authority. He commented on my breasts, so I put a bullet in his nuts." I shrug and both men groan.

Learning languages and how to be a mother wasn't just all I've done for the past nine years. Matteo insisted I be trained to protect myself; that included hand-to-hand combat, how to wield a knife, and shooting. I learned defensive driving, how to hot-wire an old car and how to launder money. Not the greatest assets to list on a resume. Luckily, being queen to the underground crime syndicate, my set of skills are perfect for this world.

Sometimes, I catch myself thinking of the familia I once had at random times. I can't help but imagine my father proud and a little intimidated at how much power Matteo has put into my hands. As for my mother, she'd be green with envy. After so many years, I've finally given in and believe my husband when he tells me she was jealous. As for Alessandro, the brother I never really had, he should be thankful he caught me back then, for now I'd slit his throat wearing a smile and my crown.

<u>Epilogue Part 2</u>

Everybody has a chapter they don't read out loud.

- justlifequotes

"Happy Birthday, mia fiore," my husband murmurs upon entering our suite. He's older now, gray hinting at his temples, yet he's still the most dominant, sinful, gorgeous man I've ever laid my eyes on.

"Thank you." I lick my lips at the sight of him in his perfectly fitted suit, polished shoes, and expertly knotted tie.

"You obeyed," he comments, eagerly staring his fill of my flesh.

"You demanded I be naked and waiting in only my diamond crown upon your arrival. It wasn't a difficult requirement as I'd most likely have thought of it myself."

He clicks his tongue at my retort. Matteo may act like my defiance drives him crazy, but looking at his slacks tells the truth. It turns him on like no other. "Stand up. Let me see what's mine." He begins to undress, momentarily sitting to untie each shoe, removing them to line them up beside the chair.

I do as he commands, eagerly awaiting his expert touch, watching him stand. Off comes the blazer, then the shirt.

"Spread your legs and open your pussy for me." His fingers unhook his slack's closure, pulling them off to fold neatly and place on the vacated chair along with this shirt and jacket. He pushes his boxer briefs down his sculpted thighs, his cock eagerly bobbing free. Someone's definitely happy to see me.

My legs slide wider, my hands gliding down to spread my lips for his enjoyment. Matteo saunters to me wearing his heated stare, and then falls to his knees before me, strong hands on my thighs as his lustful gaze trains on my core. "I love seeing you below me," I admit. It's another thing my husband goes crazy about. He never enjoys being lower than anyone, and I fully enjoy teasing him on it.

His mouth lands on my heat, tongue flicking at my bud before sucking. My thighs vibrate and I move my hands into his stylish hair. Not one lock is out of place— no doubt it's been that way all day— so I rake my fingers into it, yanking and messing it up. I love it that way when he fucks me. I like seeing him disheveled when he's always so put together. One strong hand positions my leg over his shoulder so he can have better access to my slit. He scoots under me a bit more, tongue lapping at my opening.

"Fuck," I groan as my pussy spasms. The greedy cunt is trained to his touch; I don't even attempt to fight it anymore. We've been together for far too many years for me to be able to resist his touch in any way. With his free hand he pushes two fingers deep, my body reacting exactly how he wants it to. I nearly lose my footing as I come over his hand and face.

With quick moves and his strong grip, he has me on the floor beneath him before I realize what he's done. "Mm," he groans as he takes in my breasts and legs spread wide on either side of his thighs. His cock juts out and my mouth waters, wanting his member between my lips so I can bring him to his knees again. "My love, you are stunning like this."

"Naked, in a diamond crown?" I ask as he leans up, tilting my pelvis to take him without applying pressure to my stomach.

"Underneath me with your belly swollen, wearing only diamonds. Your skin flushed having just come and at my command, ready to be fucked."

My lids droop. He's such a damn pig, but I love every bit of it. He knows exactly what to say to have me dripping wet for him. He drives in, seating his cock to the hilt, making me cry out and relishing in the sound of my delighted whimpers. "That's it, fuck me, Matteo. I've missed your big cock."

His hips swivel, one hand holding my thigh in place as the other reaches out to palm my breast. Milk leaks from them and he's groaning at the sight. It turns out, my husband has a weakness after all. When it comes to me being the mother of his children, he doesn't find anything sexier, and my body changes indicating that I carry his child has him coming left and right, praising my beauty. "So, so stunning, my love." His thumb flickers over my taught nipple before moving to play with the opposite.

"You feel so good," I moan, and he thrusts, his rhythm quick and deep, jiggling my boobs with the movements. His thumb finds my clit, pushing down until my core is clamping down on his length, and I'm not sure how much more I can take before giving into his blissful assault.

"I brought you something," he murmurs. "I'll tell you as soon as you come. Be a good girl." He flicks my clit again and I give in, too excited to see what else he could have for me. Maybe it's one of those new wedge pillows I wanted or that special table that has a hole cut out for my tummy so he can go at it hard from behind. That's my favorite position but it's difficult being so pregnant and he's far over going easy on me when I'm begging for it. I scream his name as I explode around his cock, wishing I could lean up and scrape my sculpted nails over his muscular chest. As soon as this baby is out, I'll be tearing him to pieces, leaving my marks behind.

His thrusts turn choppy as his orgasm nears, and he calls out, "Come in," right as he begins pumping me full of his hot cum. Matteo's words have my gaze trained on the doorway. It opens, a bulky shadow filling the space. The man steps inside our suite, closing the door behind him, and I gasp.

My birthday gift...Each year from Matteo has been one of his brothers. Surprising, I know. I was shocked. One night with a different brother each year; otherwise, he never shares me with a soul. He must know how much I loved being with them all and trusts me to give me such a gift.

Matteo pulls out of my core, his cum leaking from my slit as he grins down at my shocked expression. "Dante came home with me. Happy Birthday, mia Violetta. Enjoy yourself," he says and heads to the en suite bathroom to shower.

Dante takes a step closer and I swallow. He gazes at me like a man starved, a man ready to worship the Queen...

Keep Up With Sapphire:

Website:

www.authorsapphireknight.com

BookBub:

https://www.bookbub.com/profile/sapphire-knight

Twitter:

https://twitter.com/sapphireknight3

Instagram:

http://instagram.com/authorsapphireknight

Newsletter:

bit.ly/SKnightNewsletter

Facebook:

https://www.facebook.com/AuthorSapphireKnight

59128766R00113

Made in the USA
Columbia, SC
02 June 2019